THE CUBAN

A NIGEL LOGAN ACTION NOVELLA

KIRK S. JOCKELL

THE FREE MULLET PRESS, LLC

Copyright © 2021 by Kirk S. Jockell

All rights reserved.

Published by The Free Mullet Press, LLC

ISBN: 978-1-963656-09-1 (paperback version)

Book Design by The Free Mullet Press, LLC

Cover Design by The Free Mullet Press, LLC

Cover Image by MiroNovak from iStock Photos

Author Photo by Debbie Hooper Photography

The Cuban is a work of fiction. Names, characters, places, and incidents, except where indicated, are either products of the author's imagination or used fictitiously. Any resemblance to actual events or locales or persons, living or dead, is strictly coincidental. No portion of this book may be reproduced in any form without written permission from the publisher or author, except as permitted by U.S. copyright law.

For all the subscribers–old and new–of my monthly newsletter (well... almost monthly). Thank you for joining me and coming along on this journey. I appreciate you being there.

Kirk S. Jockell

Chapter 1
Chapter One

Nigel Logan is a likable and easygoing fella, even to the very few familiar with his past. There are others, though, that consider him a killer. He hates that label and tries not to think about it, which is often easier said than done. It conjures up the notion of someone cold, uncaring, and without a conscience or a measurable appreciation of life. Someone to avoid and fear. He would be the first to tell you. *I'm not that person, not really.* But what killer wouldn't? Luckily, others know him better. They know him for what he truly is—someone capable of killing, but not one that just goes around doing it. There is a difference. However, there was this one time.

***

It was a steamy summer night in his new hometown of Port St. Joe, Florida. It was early August and boiling hot, like... *Amazon Jungle* hot. Yeah, that's how to describe it. The humidity must have been ninety-three percent. It was after midnight. The sun was still hours away from the horizon. The darkness provided little relief from the ninety-six-degree temperatures felt earlier that afternoon. Mixed in the sultry air was the salt of the Gulf of Mexico. You could taste it on the tip of your tongue.

He was lost in sleep down below on his sailboat, *MisChief*, a classic 1966 Pearson Vanguard. Deep in slumber, he was oblivious to the heat and slick coating of sweat that covered his skin.

Still the new guy in town, he was figuring things out and making his way. As a retired Navy Chief Petty Officer (CPO), he sailed out of Norfolk, Virginia to remove himself from those that thought the worst of him. He wasn't running. He wasn't hiding. He was just going. There's a difference there too.

Aside from the ships the navy had stationed him on, *MisChief* was the only home he had ever known. The houses he grew up in as a kid didn't count. They were just boxes. He used to think of them as home, but when he got his first boat, that all changed. It was a Sunfish, and whether he sailed it around or just sat on her at the dock, he never felt more *at home*. It didn't take him long to figure out he was part of a special breed. Boat people.

Anyway... He was asleep, dead to the world, dreaming of quiet nothings. Then, in the faraway valleys of his self-induced coma, a faint, rhythmic thumping entered his head. At first, it was like a distant heartbeat, adding to the calmness of the night. However, as the cadence drew closer and louder, the sound of brass horns and maracas joined the percussion. It grew louder and louder until his eyelids and lips twitched in time with the music. He found himself in a dream, in a nightclub with Latin salsa music that echoed through his bones. He wanted to wake up, but couldn't. Then he realized it was no dream at all. He lay awake, looking at the overhead of his boat, feeling every note of the dance music coming through the hull. The music was so loud that nobody heard him when he yelled, "What the fuck!"

Again, he would be the first to tell you, *I'm no killer*. But on that night... He was ready to live up to that reputation.

THE CUBAN

He crawled out of the v-berth and made his way through the boat and went topside. A big, strange trawler had pulled into the slip next to him. Music was blaring from the outside speakers. Girls in bikinis, some topless, danced on the aft deck and up on the flying bridge. It was unbelievable, and his head pounded.

He stepped off *MisChief* and made his way over to the trawler. The girls dancing on deck saw him and laughed and giggled as their feet and bodies never missed a beat. Nigel found none of it amusing. They backed away and gave him plenty of room when he stepped aboard and asked, "Where is the skipper?"

The music was so loud the girls saw his lips moving, but that was all. Hell, he couldn't hear his own words. It only made him more furious. Inside the cabin, he saw more girls dancing and a single male pouring drinks in the galley. He went inside and drew more curious stares. One girl got the guy's attention with a nudge and pointed. Nigel walked toward him, and the guy looked at him up and down. When Nigel felt close enough, he raised his voice and said, "Turn it off."

The guy in the galley smiled and did a little dance. That's when Nigel lifted the snub-nosed .38 caliber revolver and pointed it at the stereo. This time he yelled, "I said, 'Turn it off!'"

There was screaming. Some girls hit the deck. Nigel walked toward the stereo and pulled back the hammer. He was getting ready to pull the trigger, but the guy shot it first with his remote. The music stopped, but the rhythm continued in his brain. Decocking the revolver, he lowered his weapon, turned toward the guy, and said, "Thank you."

As Nigel walked away toward the door, the guy laughed. Then he said, "Señor! I like you. Come again."

Nigel stopped and turned around.

With an enormous smile on his face, the guy said, "But next time... wear clothes!"

Nigel looked down at himself. Yes, he was naked. A naked man with a gun. He hadn't even realized that he pulled the weapon from its drawer until he saw it in his hand. Nigel looked back up at the guy that was still smiling. Then he turned away, went back to *MisChief*, and crawled back into the v-berth.

CHAPTER TWO

He wasn't sure how much longer he slept, but it didn't matter. As soon as his internal clock flashes 0400, his brain says, "Get up!" It's an old navy habit. Regardless of what time he goes to bed, at 4 a.m. the eyes open and his feet hit the deck.

After putting water on the stove for coffee, he went topside to the cockpit to sit in the still, thick coastal air. He sat there with his eyes closed, thinking of the crazy dream that kept running through his head. It all seemed so vivid and real. Then his eyes sprang open when a deep Latin voice said, "Hello, my new friend. I am sorry about earlier. Could I interest you in a cup of Cafecito? Cafe Cubano?"

Nigel turned his head and starkly realized, for a second time, he *hadn't* been dreaming. He stared at the guy from his dream. He sat on the aft deck of his trawler, smoking a cigar. With no breeze to speak of, the smoke made a singular column to the heavens and disappeared into the darkness.

"Please," he said, "come. Let me make you a coffee."

"Well," Nigel said, "I was just heating my water..."

Cutting Nigel off, the guy interrupted. "Nonsense! I insist. It is the least I can do."

"If you insist. Let me go below and turn my water off."

When Nigel stood, he could better see the aftermath of the trawler party. The dancing girls were scattered about the decks. All with thin, pretty smiles on their faces. A few remained on the flying bridge, their arms draped over the side of the deck. The guy saw Nigel note the scattered girls and said, "Yes. You will need to do two things."

"And what's that?"

"Be careful not to step on any of the ladies. They are exhausted, in great need of rest, and perfectly happy to sleep off their good time where they are."

"And the second thing?"

He smiled, took a long pull on his cigar, and slowly exhaled. Then he chuckled and said, "Put on pants."

Nigel got comfortable in one of the big deck chairs toward the stern and watched and studied the guy as he made his way out of the salon, around the girls, and toward the back of the boat. He was solid, probably six feet tall, with a muscular build and in good physical condition. Nigel estimated his age to be in his mid-to-late fifties. A firm chin supported his perpetual smile, as he seemed to prefer a good-spirited mood. There was an obvious charm and confidence about him that seemed contagious. It didn't surprise Nigel that he could attract such a boatload of beautiful young women.

The guy handed Nigel his tiny cup of Joe and took up with the chair next to him. Nigel took a sip. It was as strong

THE CUBAN

and sweet as any Cuban coffee he had ever had. Simply the best. He glanced at all the flesh and bikinis about the deck and asked, "How many are there?"

In his good English and heavy Latin accent, he said, "I'm not sure. Eleven. Perhaps fifteen. They are pretty little dishes, aren't they?"

"Perhaps?" Nigel asked, sounding a little astonished. "You don't know how many there are? How can you be sure you haven't lost one along the way?"

He shrugged his shoulders, said nothing.

"Where are y'all coming from?"

"I left Miami and stopped over in Key West." He waved around with dangling fingers at the sleeping girls and said, "That's where I picked up this little flock of birds. They are coeds from Florida State. Sorority girls on an adventure." He stopped to admire them as they slept. "Don't they look delicious?"

"It's just a guess, but I'm sure their fathers would be so proud."

"Ha! They came down to Duval Street via the Key West Express. It's a fast boat that runs from Ft. Myers to Key West."

"I've heard of it."

"I found them a little tipsy, having a grand time, and roaming the docks. That's when I invited them on the boat. They took me up on my offer and refused to leave. They've all had a great time. When I told them I was headed to New Orleans the next morning, they all screamed, 'We want to go!' They took their turns kissing and begging me. Who was I to say no?"

"And you're going to NOLA?"

"Yes. Heading out sometime tomorrow afternoon after I settle with the dockmaster, top off with fuel, and pump out the holding tanks. Do you have any idea how much pee this many girls can generate?"

"I can imagine."

"You have no idea."

CHAPTER THREE

Later that morning, Basilio introduced Nigel to his crew of sexy deck bunnies. "Ladies," he said, "meet Nigel Logan. Some of you will remember him as our armed exhibitionist from last night."

When his face got warm and fully blushed, he said, "Yeah... Sorry 'bout last night. I was in no condition to notice I was still in the buff."

Basilio laughed and said, "Oh, my friend, I don't think an apology is in order." All the girls shook their heads with frowns. "You seem to have certain attributes that were the center of this morning's breakfast conversation." Nigel watched as the head shakes transitioned into smiling nods. Now, he was really embarrassed. Basilio concluded, "I hope I don't offend you, but *I* failed to notice anything special. So, I have to rely on the good authority of the ladies."

Nigel said nothing. Not that his tied tongue could have unfolded itself to utter a word, anyway.

Basilio patted Nigel on the back and said, "I leave them under your charge, sir. I must go see the harbormaster and settle my bill." Before leaving, he leaned in and whispered, "The first three I introduced to you have special affections for yours truly, but the rest of the field is fair game. Have fun, my friend. I may be awhile." With a wink and slap on Nigel's back, he headed down the dock.

Nigel counted. There were fourteen. Each was stunning in her own way. They all qualified as pinup girls or centerfold features of any man's magazine. Even though they seemed to enjoy the attention Nigel gave them, he felt he was staring longer than he should have. He gave his head a vigorous shake to clear his unclean thoughts and return to some sense of decency.

"So, I understand y'all are from Tallahassee? FSU?"

"Uh huh," a few of them answered.

"Your skipper says you're going to New Orleans?"

All responded with enormous smiles, a few answered in the affirmative.

"Good party boat, huh?"

From somewhere in the back of the crowd, one bunny said, "The Cuban is the best."

Another said, "That's what we call him. He's just the sweetest."

From the back of the pack, Nigel heard. "Yeah. He sure is. Dreamy."

"Dreamy, huh? Nice. What comes next? After, NOLA?"

Looks of confusion stared back at him.

"NOLA. That's short for New Orleans, Louisiana."

THE CUBAN   11

That brought back the smiles and nervous laughs. Then he asked, "So what's next? How are y'all going to get back home?"

Nigel had their mental gears turning, and the smiles faded. Their heads snapped around, looking at each other, hoping to find an answer. Little concerned conversations started amongst the group. Suddenly, Nigel was the last thing on their minds.

After stepping back aboard *MisChief*, he turned around to look. They were all on the aft deck, and their small conversations were turning into little bitter arguments. He was quite certain these beauties weren't an accurate representation of the overall female intellect at FSU. But perhaps, and he hoped, just a representation of their sorority. Before going below to get a beer, he laughed as he gave it a wild guess: Kappa Alpha Morons.

CHAPTER FOUR

After finishing his last cup of coffee, Nigel meandered up the dock toward the marina and caught Basilio coming out of the harbormaster's office. Shortly after that, Basilio's fate in Port St. Joe unfolded. Nigel coaxed him into the little marina restaurant, the Seaside Cafe, for a beer before shoving off for NOLA. As they sat at the bar, Basilio grabbed a menu and looked it over. When the barmaid brought their drafts, he slapped the counter and said, "We'll have two of the Cuban sandwiches." Then he looked over at Nigel and asked, "You do like a Cuban, I assume?"

"Sure, but..."

He shifted his focus back on the barmaid. "That settles it. Bring us each one."

After a few minutes, she slid the sandwiches in front of them and headed back to the draft station. Basilio sat there, looking at his plate. When Nigel picked up his sandwich

THE CUBAN   13

to take a bite, Basilio put his hand on his chest and said, "Don't do that." Then he called the barmaid over.

With a smile, she said, "Yes, sir? Can I get you another beer?"

"What are these?" asked Basilio, pointing at the sandwiches. He had a distraught frown stretched across his face.

The question confused the young server. She looked down at the sandwiches, then back at Basilio. "I'm sorry, sir. I could have sworn you ordered Cuban sandwiches." She was sure of it, actually; the puzzled look on her face was unsettling to Basilio as she asked, "Is it not alright? Is there something else I can get for you instead?"

Basilio rattled off a mumbling rant in Spanish, which another couple further down the bar picked up on and understood. They exchanged glances between themselves and laughed under their breath. Then Basilio asked, "So, this is what you call a Cuban sandwich?"

The barkeep said nothing.

"This thing here. This common ham sandwich is what you call a Cuban? Get me your management, please."

She explained the manager wasn't in. Basilio looked around the small dining space and found another group of folks, some of whom had ordered the Cuban as well. Basilio got up and approached them. He introduced himself and apologized on behalf of the Cuban people. "This is so embarrassing. What you are eating is shit, not a true Cuban sandwich. Having been born in Cuba," he held his palms to his chest, "I am ashamed of this establishment. Please, let me pay for your lunch today, and if you have the time, I will happily prepare you a proper meal."

Basilio quickly turned towards the barmaid and demanded, "Take me to your kitchen. This very instant! Immediately!"

"Sir, you are upsetting the customers, and I cannot allow you back in the kitchen."

The only people upset were the barmaid and Basilio. Everyone else enjoyed the drama, and Basilio fed off that energy.

"Mierda Del Toro!" he said. "That is bullshit, I say."

Nigel grabbed his beer and followed as Basilio brushed past her to find the kitchen himself.

He stormed into the space and found a young guy working the grill. Basilio was firm but kind and benevolent. "What is your name, son?"

The kid wiped his greasy hands on his greasy t-shirt and said, "Teddy."

"Today, Teddy, you will learn the ways of a proper kitchen. Do you like your job?" Basilio asked.

The kid shrugged his shoulders and said nothing.

"Hmmm!" Basilio said, disappointed by the kid's response. "The job of any cook is to be an artist. You will either become an artist, or you will go home. So, pay attention. Now, let me see your bread."

Teddy pointed at a tall rack against the wall. Basilio walked over to inspect the inventory. He quickly shook his head and looked at Nigel. "Is there a bakery near?"

"The Piggly-Wiggly has a bakery. They are just up the street."

"Do they make Cuban bread?"

"As a matter of fact, they do."

He pulled a wad of hundred-dollar bills out of his pocket, peeled one off, and handed it to Nigel. "Here, my friend, help Basilio. Run, be fast, and get me some bread."

"Sure... how many loaves?"

"All of them! Now hurry, please."

Basilio delivered the first set of sandwiches to the table that had patiently, and with great curiosity, waited for their new sandwiches. He stood by the table and watched as everyone took their first bite. Their response resulted in no surprise in Basilio. They loved the sandwiches and told him they were the best. Basilio nodded in affirmation, then turned to the rest of the patrons and announced, "Today, it is free Cuban sandwiches for everyone. Order what you like, but your Cuban will be free, on the house." Then he looked at the barmaid and asked, "Señorita, what is your name? What do I call you?"

"Teresa, Teresa Banks. Round here, they just call me Tee."

"Very nice. I like it. A pretty name for a pretty girl."

She smiled and blushed.

"Tee, I will be very busy and need more beer. Please bring me another, but not before you take care of the other customers."

Tee said, "I don't think Pete is going to be happy about all this."

"Who is this Pete?"

Nigel piped up. "He's the manager."

"Yeah," Tee confirmed. "He should be here soon. And who is going to pay for all this?"

"Señorita," he said, "Basilio Valdez is paying for all this. You need not worry. Just keep up with the tickets. And when your manager arrives, tell him I wish to speak with him immediately."

Tee laughed. Then she reached down into the cooler, grabbed a cold gooseneck, popped the top, and slid it down the bar like a pro. Basilio grabbed it, quietly toasted her with a nod, and disappeared into the kitchen.

By the time Pete arrived, Basilio and his new protégé had not only prepared new sandwiches for the earlier patrons, but they had also already prepared sandwiches for several others and were making more.

The double doors swung open, and Pete Washington stopped just inside the door, hands on his hips. "What the hell is going on? Who are you, and what are you doing in my kitchen?"

Basilio turned to size Pete up. Pete was a young guy, pale, with red hair, rosy cheeks, and sporting a half-ass attempt at a goatee. He looked to be about twenty-five years old, but his chubby physique made him seem younger. He was as wide as he was tall. Basilio thought, *when your gym coach said get into shape, I don't think "round" is what he had in mind*. Basilio studied Pete's commanding stance and saw right through it for what it was, a feigned attempt to exude confidence and control. It was a weakness that Basilio would play to... but not take advantage of.

"Ah! You must be Master Pete. I've been waiting to meet you, sir. There is so much to discuss."

THE CUBAN

"I don't know who you are," said Pete, "but you need to get the hell out of my kitchen, like right now."

"Now Pete," Basilio said in a disappointed tone, "that is no way to thank the man that has, in one day, turned your little cafe around. You now serve the best Cuban sandwich on the Florida Panhandle! Try it!" Basilio slid a plate toward him.

"I don't give a shit about any of that," said Pete, looking at the sandwich. "All I understand is that you have taken over my restaurant and kitchen, and you are giving away my food. Now get out!"

"Oh, so you are not just a manager. You are the owner, too? Very good. But never give food away. You will make no money like that. You should talk to your customers. They are verrrry happy and love *your* new sandwich. Please. Taste it or you will hurt my feelings."

Pete got frustrated. This man in the kitchen wouldn't yield; he wouldn't leave. This strange man just continued to talk as if nothing were wrong, talking about the future and other possibilities.

Pete walked over to the phone on the wall and took it off the hook. "Okay, dammit! I've had it. No, I do not own the restaurant; I just manage it. But I'll be calling the owner right after I call the police."

"Ha! There is no need to call the police," said Basilio. "They have already been here, and they too love the sandwich."

Basilio looked Pete square in the eye, and in a softer, more serious tone said, "If you do not own the restaurant and cannot decide as its manager, perhaps it is the owner I should speak with. Please, call this owner and inform him that Basilio Valdez requests an audience."

Pete didn't like the sounds of that. He wasn't willing to admit that he couldn't decide, or that he wasn't in control, even though he wasn't. Not anymore, anyway. Instead, he hung up the phone and walked out of the kitchen and into the dining area to look at the customers. Basilio followed and placed a hand on Pete's shoulder and spoke to the room. "Ladies and gentlemen, tell Master Peter what you think about *his* new sandwich!"

The accolades rolled in from the tables. *The best. Outstanding. None better. Best sandwich ever. I want another one.*

Basilio leaned forward and quietly said to Pete, "You see. You are a genius."

Pete looked up and said, "Yeah... I guess I am. Huh?"

CHAPTER FIVE

Basilio chartered a tour bus for the next day to pick up the girls and take most of them home to Tallahassee. The others, with cars still down at the Key West Express, would go to Fort Myers. Nigel was there to witness the dramatic scene made by the girls before boarding the bus. Not wanting to go, they were crying and kissing and hugging Basilio. A few came over and kissed Nigel as well. In a whisper, one asked if he wanted to go along. He told her he would love to, but it just wasn't possible. She poked out her bottom lip in a pout of disappointment, then snapped around to wrap her arms around Basilio's neck.

"Ladies. Ladies," he said. "It is time to go. We must get a move on."

He stood by the bus door and helped each one of them board with an affectionate pat on the rump. They liked the attention. When the last one got on the bus, he looked at the driver and said, "Take good care of my little angels. Do you understand?" The driver gave a salute and closed the door.

Nigel stood watching with amazement. Basilio was old enough to be any of their fathers, but neither he nor the girls seemed to care. Some might find it a little creepy, but strangely, it wasn't. It all seemed very natural and normal; everyone was happy, and who could argue with that?

As the bus pulled away, the girls were hanging out the windows, waving and blowing more kisses. When the bus made the turn and disappeared, Basilio turned to Nigel and said, "Could I interest you in a rum? Some Havana Club?"

"Real Havana Club? From the motherland?"

"Is there any other?"

"How do you get your hands on that?"

His answer was a mischievous smile and a quick wink.

And that is how Nigel's friendship with Basilio Valdez began. That was almost two years ago. His Grand Banks 42, *Cubano Freedom,* are regular fixtures of the marina and waterfront, and he's still around: hanging out, drinking beer and rum, telling stories of Havana, and threatening to leave at a moment's notice. If you ask how long he plans to stick around, he is quick to report, "I am only a transient. Just passing through." After a few too many cocktails, he has often told Nigel, "I'm pulling out with the morning tide. I need to get an early start. Folks are waiting for me in New Orleans."

Over time, Nigel has said goodbye to his friend probably fifteen or twenty times, but now he just smiles, huffs, and ignores his threats of leaving. He may go one day, but no one at the marina expects it to be too soon. Truth is, he is like most everyone else. He has found a comfortable place. He likes it here. The people are friendly, and he fits. After this much time, it would be hard to imagine the marina without Basilio.

Having the best Cuban sandwich on the Forgotten Coast came by no accident. Basilio owns several of the best, most authentic Cuban restaurants from Ft. Lauderdale to Key West. If the Cuban sandwich being served at the Seaside Cafe was any sign, the food he served down on the keys had to be incredible. And he is quick to tell you there are no better Cuban restaurants anywhere, including Havana. Humility isn't his finest personal trait.

One late evening, they sat on the afterdeck of *Cubano Freedom,* sipping Havana Club over ice and lime. *He seemed to have an endless supply.* He held his glass toward the stars and said, "I love this view. You don't get a night sky like this in Miami. The damn city lights wash the stars out."

"Yeah, it never gets old."

He leaned his head over and asked, "Are you staying on the boat tonight?"

Lifting his glass. "That depends on how many more of these I have."

"Ha! So true."

A few months back Nigel had made one of the biggest decisions of his life, to put down some roots. For the first time in his adult life, he had an actual dwelling, a small cottage known as the *Blown Inn*. It's a simple two bedrooms with a bath. If you pull hard on the measuring tape, the entire square footage might be eight hundred. It's the perfect size with reasonable rent. He also bought an old four-wheel-drive Ford F-150 to get around town with. Walking gets old after a while.

He still spends most nights on the boat, but he also enjoys having a place to stretch out. The best feature is the screened-in porch. It is nice to sit outside and not get your ass eaten alive by mosquitos and yellow flies.

On the back of *Cubano Freedom*, they didn't have to worry about bugs. A nice sea breeze flowed across the stern. It was comfortable. As they sat there, Nigel noticed an old wooden bucket that sat off to the side. He got up and walked over for a closer inspection, then looked back at Basilio and asked, "May I?"

"Yes, my friend, but please be careful. It is ancient."

Nigel gently lifted it. The construction was strong and tight. They made the bottom of thick, clear glass. He looked back, and Basilio answered his inquisitive look. There was a hint of pain in his voice. "It is a sponge glass. It belonged to Grandfather." He sighed and continued, "I keep it near, as a reminder of the old ways."

Nigel eased it back on the deck, returned to his seat, and said nothing. After a period of quiet, Basilio shared his story.

THE CUBAN

"I grew up on the southern coast of Cuba, in the tiny fishing village of Batabanó. We were very poor. The people there still are." He looked at Nigel with a slight smile and continued, "But it wasn't always that way." He pointed at the bucket. "That was once a tool of economic prosperity. I have several, but it took me years to get that one."

He went silent for a while, and Nigel said nothing.

He finally looked over and said, "My grandfather told me stories. It all happened before I was born. The Gulf of Batabanó was once a major region for the harvest and export of sea sponges. 'None finer!' he would say with great pride. They shipped sponges all over the world, especially to the United States. The market and demand for sponges were incredible. Unlike other places where harvesters had to dive, the gulf is rather shallow. My grandfather would take his boat and crew, along with that bucket, and go out on the water. With the glass in the water, he could look down through the bucket and spot the sponges on the sea floor. With a long rake-like tool, he would harvest only the best sponges and fill up the boat." He laughed out loud and said, "My grandfather said that by the time the boat was full, and they made it back to the dock, the boat smelled of an old whore." He was quiet again until he said, "But that was okay. He loved that smell. It meant money and food to feed hungry mouths."

Nigel asked, "Did your father harvest sponges?"

"Oh yes, once he became of age, he was out there alongside my grandfather. Until..." Some of the color left his face and the look of pain filled in.

"Basilio. I am sorry. I didn't mean to pry. I just..."

He interrupted. "It's okay, my friend. These things I feel I can share... with you... not everyone... but you, yes."

To have earned enough of his trust, that Basilio felt comfortable sharing intimate details of his life and history flattered Nigel, but he said, "That is fine. I am honored, but it isn't necessary. Please don't feel you have to tell me anything."

He smiled. "It isn't a matter of *having* to tell you. It's that I *can* tell you."

Nigel wasn't sure what he meant by that, but if Basilio wanted to talk, he'd be the friend that listened. But rather than continuing, Basilio stood, picked up the glasses, and said, "Too much talking. Not enough rum. Let me freshen our glasses."

He came back with the drinks and two cigars. Nigel accepted the rum and graciously declined the hand-rolled tobacco. "Are you sure?" Basilio asked. "They are of the finest leaves."

"And not from the Dominican Republic, if I had to guess."

Before sitting back in his chair, Basilio gave Nigel a grunt and a *don't be stupid* look. Nigel smiled. After getting comfortable again, he offered the cigar once more and Nigel declined it again. He lit his and pulled on it hard until the end was burning red hot. The aromatic smoke filled the air. Having been a CPO in the navy, Nigel knew what cheap, nasty cigars smelled like. This was anything but. With his drink in one hand and his cigar nestled between the fingers of his other, Basilio settled back and relaxed. Nigel took a nice sip from his glass, and Basilio did the same.

THE CUBAN

He didn't go to sleep, but Nigel had his eyes closed for a good while. They were sharing a nice evening in good company, but his eyes popped open when he heard, "There were two things that changed everything. First was the development and wide production of the artificial sponge. My grandfather's sea sponges were no longer needed. Yes, he still had some exports to Europe, but in time those dried up as well. He was out of business."

Nigel said nothing and let Basilio continue. "Then there was the revolution. According to my grandfather, times were already tough under Batista's rule. The lucrative sponge business meant hefty taxes, but at least there was enough left over to make for a decent living. Once the sponge exports dried up, Batista fell out of love with the region. However, that didn't give him cause to ease up on the taxation. That was the thing about Batista. If you made him money, he loved you. If you didn't, you were the scum of the earth."

"And Castro?"

"Ahhh... That was a unique problem, as I'm sure you are aware. Yes, things improved at first with education and healthcare, but it was all at the high cost of human rights. Plus, there was the issue with my uncle."

"Your uncle?"

"I never met him. He worked under the Batista regime. According to my grandfather, he didn't like his job. He secretly didn't like Batista, but it was a job, and it trapped him. You couldn't just quit, but perhaps he should have taken his chances. After Castro came to power, they rounded up many that worked under Batista and put them on trial. They later executed him along with hundreds of others. Grandfather told me they killed a good man.

"They outraged my father with the death of his brother. Oh, how he hated Castro. He secretly organized an underground movement to oppose the Castro regime and its repressive policies. According to my grandfather, Father often spoke of the impossible task of assassination. My grandfather warned him against such talk, but my father wouldn't listen. One evening while meeting with three other dissidents, armed soldiers stormed our home and took him and the others away. I never saw my father again. It is one of my first memories as a child. I was very young."

Nigel watched as he filled his mouth with cigar smoke and exhaled. Then he followed it with a sip of rum. He turned his head to look at Nigel, and with a smile said, "I am sorry to bore you with such details."

"Yes, boring. That's what your family history is, a real bore. Don't be stupid."

He laughed, took another drink, and said, "It was a long time ago."

"Basilio, you don't have to answer this question, but I have to ask. How did you end up in the United States?"

He looked off into the distance with raised eyebrows and thought about the question before speaking.

"As I told you, we were poor. After they took my father, my mother and I had to live with my grandfather. We fished to make a living. I say we; I helped my grandfather when I could. I spent most of my time in school or studying. All I wanted to do was fish and help, but neither my mother nor grandfather would allow it. They told me my

THE CUBAN

education was more important than anything. I studied hard, to get smart and to make time to help on the boats.

"Later, as a young man, I helped my grandfather full time. They wanted me to go to university, but my grandfather was getting old and growing weaker and needed my help. I told them it was only temporary, but I had no plan to leave. When I was nineteen, my mother became ill with cancer. I could not help my grandfather because I had to care for my mom. We needed money... so I did something stupid."

He took a long sip of his rum and said, "There was an old, abandoned government building just outside of town. I would break in and take copper tubing from the plumbing, to sell it on the black market. It was quick money... until they caught me and sentenced me to eight years in prison."

"Eight years...? Son of a bitch."

"And I can promise you, eight years in a Cuban prison is like a lifetime. That was in 1978. Two years later, I wasn't even aware of the date. The guards came and loaded many of us on buses. We thought were going to be executed. However, they drove us to the Port of Mariel..."

"So, you were part of the infamous boat lift?"

"Exactly. They filled the boat beyond capacity. There was barely room to move. Like sardines, they packed us in and said good riddance. When the seas got rough in the Gulf Stream, I didn't think we would make it. But we did."

Nigel's eyes wandered to the sponge bucket, and he asked, "How is it you could take possession of your grandfather's bucket?"

He looked at Nigel and said nothing.

"Basilio, earlier you said something about how you felt you *could* tell me things, but not to others. What did you mean by that?"

"We are not so much different, me and you."

"I don't understand."

"We both have pasts that are better served staying a part of our history. Wouldn't you agree?"

Nigel said nothing, thinking, *What does he know about me?*

"We seem to have a common trait."

"And that would be?"

He held his glass of rum toward Nigel and said, "To do whatever needs to be done, regardless of the price or consequences."

Nigel held his stare and smile for a short while, then said, "So, I guess you looked into my past?"

"Yes, but please, do not be offended. It is important that I know about the people I care about."

Nigel gave a slight nod and reached out with the rim of his glass. When the fine crystal touched and rang out, Basilio said, "You never know when you might need an ally."

"Basilio, I'm not sure how much you know, and I don't care, but the folks around here know nothing of my past. I'd like to keep it that way. As for needing an ally, let us hope that is never the case."

They agreed and toasted one last time before knocking back the rum.

CHAPTER SIX

A few days later, Nigel was at the cottage. The grass needed mowing, and he can't stand the idea of the place not looking shipshape. After he cut the St. Augustine and weeds to the same height, it was time to hop in the truck and run down to the marina. *MisChief's* diesel engine needed an oil change. Already sweaty and grubby, there was no time like the present to get it done.

He grabbed the driver's side door handle of his truck and noticed he had left the window rolled down. Then he noticed the hitchhiker. Sticking his head in the cab, he said, "Now, what the hell are you doing in there?" It was a local feral cat that had been hanging around. Nigel calls him Tom. Pretty original, huh? Tom sat on the passenger side. A squirming shrew dangled and squealed for mercy as it hung from his grinning mouth. The cat got up and walked across the front seat. Nigel took a step back and opened the door. "Take that shit somewhere else. The truck is off-limits. You hear me?" The cat came bouncing out. It never looked back, and Nigel watched as Tom dashed off to some secret destination of torture. Stepping up into the truck, he said, "Make it a quick kill, Tom." *Damn cat.*

Once at the marina, it surprised Nigel to hear the big booming voice of Basilio. He had been out of town on business, and Nigel did not expect him back so soon. He was on the outside deck of the Seaside Cafe, yucking it up with tourists. Whenever Basilio speaks, his location is no secret. You can hear him a mile away.

Nigel bounced down the steps toward the docks when a big voice got his attention. "Nigel, my friend. Stop."

Nigel turned around and, while walking backward, said, "I have boat work to do, and I thought you were out of town."

"Nonsense. Come. Just for a minute. I want you to meet some people."

"Just for a minute."

Nigel trotted over to where Basilio stood with a young couple. Extending a hand to the guy, he said, "Hello. I'm Nigel Logan." He gave the young lady a nod and a smile.

"Nice to meet you," said the young man.

"Ha!" Basilio laughed in Nigel's ear. "These are the Wilsons from Ohio. And while I am sure it thrills them to make your acquaintance; this isn't who I want you to meet. Come with me."

They excused themselves from the Buckeyes and headed toward the restaurant. "Damn, Basilio. What smells so good?"

He stopped at the door, closed his eyes, and inhaled through his nose as he smiled. "It is heaven, my friend. Culinary heaven... let me show you."

THE CUBAN

They went inside, and the aromas grew even stronger. Basilio moved quickly across the floor, as Nigel noticed an unfamiliar girl helping the wait staff deliver food. She was of Latin descent with long, shapely legs. Her dark brown eyes shone brightly beneath matching eyebrows, as her full, colorful lips, void of lipstick, held a radiant smile. It was all framed by her wavy, shoulder-length hair. She was gorgeous.

The desperate and joyous thoughts of changing the oil on *MisChief* seemed to disappear. Now he was more concerned about his smelly state and appearance. He grabbed the front of his t-shirt and pulled it up to his nose. *Damn.* Then he grabbed Basilio by the arm. "Hey! Stop, dammit. Quit being in such a hurry." He finally got Basilio's attention, and he stopped. "Who is she?"

"Ah, my friend. You like?"

"What's not to like?"

"You better be careful. Your girlfriend might not like the attention you are giving Isabel."

"Isabel? That's her name? Wait... girlfriend...? You mean Candice? Oh, she's not my girlfriend. We're good friends. That's all."

"That's not the way she tells it."

"She would like our friendship to be more, but it simply isn't a good idea. I don't think I have to tell you why."

"Ah... the skeletons."

"Drop it. Now, who is she?"

"Her name is Isabel Rivas. Let me get her."

Nigel did another test smell of his t-shirt. *Crap!*

Basilio got her attention, waved her over, and said something in Spanish that Nigel took as an introduction since it included his name.

She reached out. Nigel gently took her hand. She nodded, and with great, deliberate effort, said, "I am very pleased to meet you."

"Very good, Isabel," said Basilio. He looked at Nigel and said, "That was good, wasn't it, Nigel?"

"That was just awesome. Whatever you say."

Basilio said something to her again in Spanish. She nodded and said, "OooohKay!"

Nigel couldn't take his eyes off her, and he followed her every movement as she hurried back into the kitchen. He looked at Basilio and said, "I like everything about that. I mean everything."

"Well, my friend, there might be one little detail you won't like."

"Impossible. What could that possibly be?"

"Her husband. You get to meet him next."

"Husband?" Nigel followed him to the kitchen. "A husband, really? You're shitting me, right? That part's just a joke. You're pulling my leg. Please, tell me you're kidding."

When they came through the double doors, Basilio said something in Spanish and a fit, handsome Latino guy in a cook's apron turned and came their way. Again, the introduction was in Spanish, but unlike Isabel's successful stab at English, he only offered a nod and a smile. Basilio then looked at me and said, "This is Alvaro Rivas, Isabel's husband..."

"Stop with the husband thing, will ya? You're killing me."

THE CUBAN   33

"Alvaro is my newest chef. The very best of Cuban cuisine. He is the reason the place smells so wonderful."

Alvaro said something to Basilio, and his Spanish held a hint of urgency. Basilio was quick to answer with a wave of his fingers. "Si, yes, go. Go."

The young cook hurried back to the stove.

"He is cooking Vaca Frita, sweet plantains, and black beans. Oh... it is so good. Wait until you taste it."

They went back into the restaurant and took a seat at the bar.

"What are they doing here?" Nigel asked.

"I am still out on business. Between you and me, we are just passing through on our way to New York City. I am loaning Alvaro to a friend of mine while things calm down. He has a restaurant there and desperately needs a talented chef. Little does my friend know, but he is getting the best."

"Until things calm down?"

"Forget that. Just a figure of speech."

Figure of speech. What the hell was that supposed to mean? Not that he cared. He had other things on his mind. "Is Isabel going too? I mean, she could..."

Basilio laughed out loud, interrupted, and said, "Stop, my friend. Stop. Don't do this to yourself. No, she is not staying."

"Crap."

About that time Isabel came out carrying food to a table. She looked at the two of them and gave a happy, friendly smile. Basilio and Nigel watched as she floated across the floor, delivered the food, and drifted back to the kitchen. They both had been holding their breath without realizing it. As she disappeared behind the door, they both let out a deep sigh. Then they looked at each other and laughed.

CHAPTER SEVEN

Nigel sat atop his throne, Stool Seventeen, at the Reid Avenue Bar and Bottle Shop, better known as the City Bar. It was full of locals. A gaggle of guys waited their turn to challenge the winners from one of the two pool tables in the back. Nigel gazed into his empty mug when he felt someone drop onto the stool next to him. It was his good friend, Red.

Red was the first friend he made after getting into town. Wait... that's not true. The first friend he made was the sexy, shapely blond with purple streaks, pulling beers behind the bar, Candice. The very Candice that Basilio referenced as his girlfriend.

When he first made landfall in Port St Joe, he dropped a hook and came ashore looking for something to eat. The City Bar was his first stop, and he made a not-so-healthy meal of bourbon and Chex Mix. Not an excellent combination. Later that evening, after being fueled up and ready for anything, an altercation broke out with a local. Nigel knocked him out, then passed out. Sweet Candice kept him out of jail. It's a relationship only found in fairy tales. The next morning, he woke up on Red's couch with one of the worst hangovers he could remember.

Red said, "Candice! Please get us a round when you get a chance. The usuals."

The usuals. For Nigel, that's a Coors Light with a wedge of lime. For Red, it's whatever's in the keg that serves the daily, two-dollar draft, usually Natty Light.

She pulled the drafts and delivered them with a smile. When she set Nigel's beer down, she leaned across the bar, exposing the perfect amount of cleavage, and asked, "What are you doing later tonight? Want to hang out after I close up the place?"

He lifted his head to look her in the eyes and said, "You're doing that..." He shifted his eyes down for another glance, "on purpose."

"Damn right I am. Is it working?"

"Oh yeah, it does the trick, but..."

"But, what?"

"Well..."

The idea of getting involved scared Nigel. The one thing he takes comfort in knowing is she isn't looking for a one-night stand. She's not that kind of gal. Hell, parts of him wish she were. They could go the distance for an evening or two and get it all out of their systems. The better part of him is thankful she isn't. As flirtatious and forward as she can be, she only wants someone to hold and care for her. And not just anybody, Nigel. It puzzles him why she's so determined.

THE CUBAN   37

The thing that scares him most is that she knows nothing about him or his past. It wouldn't be fair to get involved, start something good, knowing it would more than likely end with a broken heart or hearts. No, he knows what's best, and that's for her to steer clear of Nigel Logan.

"... it just isn't a good idea," he said. "Please try to understand. Be my friend, for now."

"All my guy *friends* are gay. Are you like gay or something?"

He wasn't expecting that. Never saw it coming. In the corner of his eye, he saw Red turn his way, waiting for an answer.

"What are you looking at?"

Red said nothing with a thin smile.

"Stop looking at me like that, dammit."

"Well," he said, "answer the question."

"No!"

"No, to what?" asked Red. "You're not going to answer the question, or you're not gay?"

It frustrated Nigel, and he shook his head to pull his thoughts together.

Candice prodded, "Well?"

"No! No, dammit."

"Be specific."

"No. I'm not gay!"

Everyone in the bar heard him. The room got quiet. A guy somewhere in the back broke the silence. "Well, son of a bitch. That's too bad."

Candice smiled from ear to ear. Then she got on her toes and spoke over Nigel's shoulder. "Told you, Gene. Never doubt me. Now keep your grubby hands off my man."

The entire bar busted out in a fit of laughter. Eventually, Nigel joined in. Candice leaned over the bar, kissed his cheek, and said, "Yes. I've said it before. You're a keeper."

After things settled back down, Red asked, "Did you get to taste some of that Cuban food they were serving up at the Seaside Cafe?"

"Yeah. It was the best. Crazy good."

"Well, shit!" he lamented. "I missed it. I heard it was good. Some guy Basilio knows did all the cooking."

"Yup. That pretty well sums it up."

"Where is he, anyway? Does he plan to get his guy back in the kitchen?"

"I'm not sure," he lied, "just that he'd be gone for a while and to look after his boat."

"Well, shit!"

Basilio had left with Alvaro and Isabel to New York three days earlier. He said he wasn't sure how long he would be away, and he asked Nigel to monitor *Cubano Freedom*. "Not a problem," Nigel told him. "Easy enough."

He also reminded Nigel, "And again, you are the only one that knows I am taking the kids to New York. It would be best if it stayed that way. I'm sure you can appreciate that."

Nigel figured it had something to do with whatever needed *calming down*. "Basilio, I don't know what you are talking about, and I have no idea where you are going."

He slapped Nigel on the back. "Thank you. And take good care of my girl. Start her engines now and then to keep her from getting too stale. Adios, my friend. That's Spanish."

"Arrivederci... That's Italian."

Red and Nigel closed down the bar. Candice locked the door behind them after she escorted them out and kicked them to the curb. They started down the sidewalk, and Red said, "It's a beautiful night. Smell that salt air. I love it."

Nigel closed his eyes for a beat. "Yup."

"She's a good girl, you know. And crazy about you."

"Yeah, I can tell."

"Nigel, there isn't a single guy in this town that wouldn't love to be in your shoes. What's the problem?"

Nigel stopped to look at his friend. "It's complicated."

Red kept walking. "*Complicated*. That's real original."

Looking around, Nigel noticed he was at the corner of Reid Avenue and Fourth, going the wrong way. Red kept going.

"Hey!" Nigel called after him. "I'm turning around. Going to the boat."

He answered with a thumb in the air.

"Be careful driving home."

Nigel stood there for a while and watched his friend stroll down the sidewalk. Red has an easy-going stride that makes Nigel smile. He has known a lot of special people.

Spending twenty-three years in the navy will do that for you. But... never in his life has he ever known anyone as cool, calm, and collected as Red. Always ready for a good time, but never in a hurry to get there. Hell, he's never in a hurry about anything, and chances are he will never make it home. You can bet dollars to donuts that he'll drive his Explorer onto the beach and sleep behind the wheel with the windows down.

Nigel turned and headed the other way, taking quick glances into the storefront windows of the shops as he passed. They were all dark and closed tight for the evening. The entire town shuts down this way every night. A sensation of calm filled his soul, and he felt alone, in a good way. He turned to find Red one last time, but his friend had already made the corner and disappeared. He started walking again. The town's only sounds were the flip and the flap of his flops on the sidewalk. It seemed louder than normal.

Then he realized he wasn't so alone. The street was empty of vehicles, and all the storefronts were dark, except one. Candice's Jeep, a CJ-7, sat parked in front of the bar. A faint glow came through the window and illuminated the sidewalk.

He stopped and looked through the window. Candice was behind the bar sitting on a stool, drinking a beer, and studying paperwork. A pencil in her mouth. He couldn't take his eyes off her. Her good looks are undeniable. She is sexy and knows how to exploit her strengths to generate healthy tips without being a tease or leading fellas on. Well... she might not lead a young buck into thinking he had a chance, but she sure left them wishing they had. At

THE CUBAN

that moment, though, as he watched her work alone, he noticed her deep beauty. Red's words came back to him. *She's a good girl, you know.* He had no reason to think otherwise. Smiling, he turned and continued down the sidewalk.

In the bar, Candice was tallying up receipts. For a short while, though, she found herself just staring at the paperwork, not calculating the numbers. Then, with a grin, she turned her head to look out the empty window. "No, Nigel Logan. You won't be able to ignore me, and I will make you mine. Sweet dreams." She reached for the calculator and went back to work. The smile never left her face.

CHAPTER EIGHT

He made a left at First Street and headed toward the marina, stopping at the corner before crossing Highway 98. Except for the PSJPD squad car sitting in the Advance Auto parking lot, there wasn't a vehicle in sight. After getting across, he gave the officer a friendly wave and got nothing in return. He got closer to check on him. The cop was asleep. Resting up for another action-packed night of law enforcement activity that would never come.

Back aboard *MisChief*, he sat in the cockpit to listen to the night sounds of the marina. From off the bay, a breeze flowed through the network of sailboat masts, flying bridges, and fishing towers. The gentle wind caused small wavelets to slap against the hull, and an unsecured halyard of a distant sailboat kept time as it tapped its mast, creating a nautical lullaby worthy of a good night's sleep.

He had the marina to himself. His favorite. He opted for a nightcap of bourbon before hitting the rack. His every day is Jim Beam, but he wanted something more special

THE CUBAN   43

for the occasion and reached for the Four Roses Single Barrel. With a generous, four-finger-pour in his glass, he went back up to the cockpit to nurse his drink, sipping with his eyes closed until the warmth caused his eyes to shut for good. He wasn't looking for sleep, but it found him anyway.

When his eyes opened, both hands securely held the glass in his lap. Less than a finger remained, so he lifted the glass to knock back the rest. Through the bottom of the glass, a light caught his attention. Across the basin, the cabin lights of *Cubano Freedom* were glowing. "Why, you sneaky bastard," he said aloud. "You're home."

His watch read 0230, so he grabbed the phone and dialed Basilio's number. It rang until his voicemail picked up, so he ended the call without leaving a message. Giving himself an order, he said, "Shit, Logan. It's late. Go to bed."

Down below, he set his glass in the sink. As his t-shirt hit the floor, the phone rang. It was Basilio. "Hey, man. What time did you get in?"

"What did you say, Nigel?" He was trying to talk over the party sounds of a crowded room and Latino dance music.

Nigel stuck his head up through the hatch for a look. "I said, 'What time did you get...?'"

Nigel's brain registered a reality. While not uncommon for Basilio to throw a party on his boat, there was no music coming across the water.

"Basilio, somebody is on your boat. Can you hear me? On *Cubano Freedom*."

"No hear! Dance, dance, dance. Las chicas bonita every-where!" The call ended.

"Shit!"

Nigel ducked back below, pulled open a drawer, and reached in. "Dammit!" His weapon of choice, the Beretta M9 that would normally be there, wrapped in an oiled cloth, wasn't. It was still sitting in some evidence box back in Virginia, part of a continuing investigation looking into the death of a local rapper thug. The little snub-nosed revolver would have to do. Not ideal, but effective. He closed the drawer with a slam. *Son of a bitch.*

Running in flip-flops is never a good idea, so he kicked them off the second he hit the dock. He ran fast to get around to the other dock. *Cubano Freedom* made berth at the end. As he made the turn to dash down the dock, Basilio's boat went dark, but the security lamp at the end of the dock provided adequate illumination. After a few strides, he slowed down. There was only one way off the dock. Whoever was out there would have to get by Nigel to leave. On full alert, he made quick checks of each boat as he worked down the dock. When he saw someone exit the cabin and walk aft along the side-deck, he crouched down behind a boat box. *Logan, you're crazy*, he thought. He didn't know what he was up against, and he only had five rounds in the revolver. He looked around.

The next boat over was a friend's charter boat. His name is Doc, and the boat is a nice Everglades center console, aptly named *The Doctor's Office*. When the intruder was out of sight, he kept low and slipped over the gunnel and onto the deck of Doc's boat. He's been out with Doc before, so he knew exactly where he kept his fishing priest,

THE CUBAN   45

the short, weighted club for quickly ending a fish's life. He removed it from its box; having it might come in handy. He jumped off the boat and took off, trying to stay low, move fast, and be stealthy. A tough order for someone six-foot-three and two-hundred-thirty pounds. Nigel saw another person emerged from the cabin.

"Halt!" he yelled. "Who are you? What are you doing there?"

The guy turned, saw Nigel coming, and yelled something in Spanish. Nigel picked up his pace, and he saw the guy swing his legs over the stern rail, land on the swim-platform, and disappear. Nigel jumped on *Cubano Freedom* and moved aft. "Stop. Who are you?" Now leaning against the stern rail, he saw two men sitting in a large, rigid inflatable, its well-tuned four-stroke engine humming away. "Hands where I can see them." He kept the barrel moving from one guy to another. "Don't move. Who are you? What do you want?"

They sat there in silence until the guy driving rattled off something.

"I don't speak Spanish, asshole."

Turns out he wasn't talking to Nigel, but to the third intruder that stood behind him. The last thing Nigel remembered was seeing the guy in the boat grin.

CHAPTER NINE

EMTs rolled Nigel down the dock on a gurney. His eyes took time to focus, but once they did, he saw a face looking down at him. As the wheels of the gurney rattled a melodic rhythm on the deck planking, the face said, "Well... welcome back."

Turning his head from side to side, he saw the familiar faces of his marina family gazing in as he passed. When they got to the *Doctor's Office*, Doc peeked in and said, "Take it easy, big guy."

Turning back to the face, Nigel said, "What happened?"

"You tell me. The marina staff found you as they made their morning rounds."

Another voice came into the conversation from the other side of the gurney. "What were you doing on the Grand Banks? Can you tell us what happened?"

Nigel turned his head the other way to concentrate on a new face, walking alongside and looking down. Squinting

THE CUBAN

helped with recognition. It was the napping cop from the night before.

Returning a blank stare, the cop continued. "*Cubano Freedom*. That's where they found you. What happened?"

It all came back to him, and he thought of Basilio and wondered what he should or could share. He kept it simple and truthful, mostly. "Basilio is out of town. I saw activity on his boat. I came over to investigate. Then…" With his fingers, he felt the dried blood and the grapefruit-sized knot on the back of his head. "Shit."

"Is there anything else you can tell me? Did you see who did this?"

"No, not up close," he lied. "Son of a bitch sucker punched me." A thought entered his head, which prompted a rush of panic. He tried to sit up, but the gurney straps said *no*. "Shit! My weapon. Did you find it?"

The cop lifted the revolver with two fingers. "Drop by the station later and you can pick it up."

"Thanks."

The face of the EMT chimed in. "We are taking you to the hospital for observation. The doctor will probably want a scan of your noggin."

"That is fine," said Nigel, "but what I really need right now is some Jim Beam. Can we stop by my truck on the way to the ambulance? I keep a bottle in the console for just such occasions."

"I don't think I needed to hear that," said the cop.

Nigel turned to look at him, gave a wink, and said, "Medicinal purposes."

He sat in bed, poking a plastic fork in a cup of shitty, generic-lime gelatin they brought him for lunch. The door to his room opened and a young doctor in a white lab coat entered the room and stood at the foot of the bed. *Why do they always seem to do that?*

"So, what's the verdict, Sawbones?"

He returned a snicker and said, "You have a really hard head."

"And I'm paying how much for you to tell me that?"

"You are lucky," said the doctor. "It could have been significantly worse. It's going to be sore for a while, but we saw nothing alarming that would indicate permanent damage. Like I said, 'You have a really hard head.'"

"When can I get out of here?"

"Just take it easy. Don't be in a rush. I'd like to keep you a few more hours, so the staff can monitor you. Do you have anyone you can call to take you home?"

"I'll take him home."

Both the doctor and Nigel turned their heads. Neither one of them had noticed Candice when she slipped into the room. The doctor gave Nigel a look and said, "Well, I guess that settles that. I'll leave y'all alone to visit."

After the doc exited, Nigel said, "That is sweet, but you don't have to do that. I can call Red. He would jump at the chance to come down and make fun of me."

"And you think I won't," she said with a wink.

She smiled. It was a friendly smile. A happy one. It seemed to cradle her cute nose and eyes. Then it faded away, and she asked. "What happened?"

He kept to his simple story but added, "Basically, I was stupid and sloppy. Someone sneaked up and whacked the

THE CUBAN   49

living shit out of my head. It had to be one hell of a blow.
I don't even remember it happening. Like a bedtime story
when you don't last long enough to hear the first word.
Boom! I was out."

"I'm sorry."

"Don't be. Trouble is my middle name."

"What do you mean by..."

The room phone rang and interrupted her. The receiver
was just out of his reach, so she grabbed it and answered.
She was having a delightful time with whoever was on
the other line: "Oh... he looks like shit... Yes, meaner than
ever... You know as well as I do, he's as stubborn as an ox..."

She cut Nigel a mischievous look, and he mouthed the
words, *Who is it?*

"Yes, he up to talking. He hasn't shut up since he got
here." She reached toward him with the handset, and he
took it.

"Hello."

"Ahhh, I see sweet Candice is there taking good care of
you."

"Basilio. How did you know I was here?"

"The cops called me to ask questions. I told them to clap
you in irons and toss your thieving ass in jail."

"Funny. I'm a lot of things. A thief isn't one of them."

"I know. I know."

There was something in the way he said that last, *I know*
that made an eyebrow lift.

"We have a lot to talk about, don't we?"

In the most serious tone Nigel has ever heard him use,
Basilio said, "Yes. But not in present company or on the
phone."

"So, you will bring me up to speed…" Nigel noticed Candice giving him a curious look as she listened to the conversation, so he added, "on all your travels and business trip?"

"Yes. And I will be home tomorrow. I am already headed that way."

Nigel laughed out loud, looked at Candice, and said, "Great, can't wait. Just do me a favor and leave out the inane details." Candice returned a smile. "Your stories can be quite a bore."

"I promise you, my friend. There will be nothing boring about this."

"Ha! Time will tell. Safe travels."

"See you soon and stay low. Now hand the phone back to sweet Candice."

He held the phone out. "Here, he wants to talk to you."

She took it. "Yes." She listened. She cut the occasional glance toward Nigel. A blushing face joined her thin smile, then she laughed and said, "Don't worry. I'll take better care of him than he deserves. Hurry home. Goodbye."

A cold sensation awakened Nigel as his head was being lowered on a bag of ice. His blurry eyes cleared to find Candice looking down at him. "Hello," she said with a smile.

When he went to sit up, the pain in the back of his head reminded him of what he had been through. She gently

THE CUBAN

pressed him back down on his bed. "Easy, big boy. The doctor wants you to rest and keep ice on it."

"What time is it?"

"Around midnight."

"You've been here the whole time?"

"The doctor said it would be a good idea if someone stayed with you. How are you feeling?"

"Like a truck ran over me. And..."

"What?"

"Hungry."

"That's a good sign. I checked your pantry. You're somewhat of a minimalist when it comes to stocking up on food. I found some soup. How does clam chowder sound?"

Nigel nodded.

While she was gone, he reached back, felt the back of his head, and tried to replay the events of the night before. *How could I have been so stupid to allow myself to get suckered that way?* The faces of the guys in the boat were clear as a bell. If he got a chance to see them again, recognizing them wouldn't be an issue, and he hoped to have that opportunity. Things would be different next time.

She brought bowls for each of them and helped him sit up, propping up pillows. Once he got comfy, she left and returned, carrying two bottles of cold beer. She held them up in the doorway and said, "Our first date. Not exactly what I had planned, but I'll take what I can get."

"You're a nut, girl."

The chowder hit the spot, but he found the beer was better. They ate in silence. She looked tired and had every right to be.

"Here," he said, handing over his bowl. "Thank you, very much. For everything. You should probably get on home and get some rest. I've imposed on you long enough."

"Yeah. I'm tired, but you didn't impose. Hell, taking your clothes off was well worth my time."

It was true. He was naked and hadn't realized it. "When did you do that?" he asked with a slight blush.

"After you went to sleep. I couldn't see letting you sleep in those dirty old cargo shorts."

"I'm surprised I didn't wake up."

She bit her lower lip and said, "I was verrrry slow and careful about it." Then she reached over to lift the bed sheets to peek underneath. Nigel slapped the sheet back down, and she laughed and bounced her eyebrows. "Oh... you're no fun, and besides, it isn't like I haven't already gotten an eyeful."

"Oh... for crying out loud. Stop, will ya?"

She was more tired than she knew. After a long yawn, she said, "Okay. Okay. Can I get you anything before I leave?"

"Another beer, maybe."

"Serving up beers is the thing I do best." She headed toward the door, then turned around and licked her lips. "But it isn't the very *best* thing I do. Maybe one day I'll show you."

"Just go get the beer, please. Sheesh!"

When she returned, she set the bottle down on the nightstand and he reached out and took her hand. He pulled her close, kissed her hand, and said, "I mean it. Thank you for staying with me. You didn't have to do that."

THE CUBAN

She looked at him with her beautiful eyes and said, "A kiss on the hand? Can't you do any better than that?"

"Believe me. I wish I could, but..."

She said nothing, but he was sure she could sense the desires he held for her. With her hand still in his, he wanted badly to pull her close. He wanted to kiss her and let the chips fall where they may. The moment contained all the ingredients of a perfect storm. A night of hot, sweaty, casual passion would serve him well. It had been a while since he enjoyed the carefree warmth of a wanting female. As she looked at him, he saw her communicate the same. It just wasn't smart to answer the calls of their animal instincts, solely to satisfy pent-up desires. She wanted more than he could give. And he wouldn't take advantage of her willingness to quell his sexual frustrations. That wouldn't be right.

She held his stare as the possibilities ran through her mind. Then she smiled, leaned in, and said, "It's okay, Nigel. Not tonight. I get it. I'm disappointed, but quite happy to see I'm getting your attention. That's quite a circus tent you have working under the sheet."

"Oh, crap!" Without realizing it, he had worked himself up to a state of preparedness. His tool stood ready for anything. His hand moved quickly to cover the state of his affairs, and the embarrassment that overcame him allowed for a timely deflation.

She winked, kissed him on the forehead, and said, "What a waste."

CHAPTER TEN

Nigel got a call from Basilio a couple of days later. He was at his boat and invited Nigel over. "Rum and cigars, my friend. I owe you."

As Nigel walked down the dock, he saw Basilio. He had moved a couple of big deck chairs down on the dock. A small table sat between the chairs with two glasses; a bottle of fifteen-year-old Havana Club served as a centerpiece.

"Sit! Sit!" he said. "Pour yourself a stiff drink." He held out a cigar.

Nigel waved off the leaf and took a seat. "Turn for me," he said. "Let me see the back of your head."

He did, and Basilio winced.

"Is it still sore?"

"Yes, but much better than it was." Grabbing the bottle, he added, "This won't hurt it any."

"Take all you need, my friend."

They sat in silence for a while and enjoyed the rum. Nigel broke the ice by asking about the big party Basilio

THE CUBAN   55

had attended the night he had called. His face lit up like a Christmas tree as he reported the details of the evening, the girls, and the good time. Then he said, "But... while I was having a grand time with young, sweet señoritas, you were getting your skull caved in."

"Yeah, that's one way of looking at it."

"I am sorry, Nigel. Believe me. I didn't mean for that to happen, but I guess, given the circumstances, it shouldn't surprise me."

After a long pull on his rum, Nigel said, "I believe you, and you have my full, undivided attention."

Basilio was about to say something when another man emerged from *Cubano Freedom*. He was holding up, of all things, an old-school bowling ball bag when he said something in Spanish. Basilio remained seated as the man approached and opened the bag. Basilio leaned over to look, and Nigel stretched his neck to see. Catching Nigel's curiosity, the guy tilted the bag away, and he saw nothing.

"Gracias, Desi! Thank you for coming on such short notice. This is the only one you found?"

Desi could obviously understand English. He nodded and said, "Yes, just one. A timed device connected to the ignition."

"Ahhh... so, we agree on how we must proceed?"

"Si."

"And everything is set?"

"Si."

"Sir, I continue to be forever in your debt. Thank you."

Desi nodded to both Basilio and Nigel before leaving and walking down the dock. Nigel turned his head to watch him go, and said, "What was that all about?"

"Desi is a man I often work with. A countryman and one of many talents, especially with explosives."

"Explosives!"

"Nigel, please keep your voice down. Let's go aboard and I'll explain."

"Everything?"

"Yes."

Inside the salon, Nigel found a comfortable place to sit and made sure the bottle of rum was near. After recharging his glass, he said, "Let's have it."

"You have been enjoying the Cuban food that I've brought here. Have you not?"

"Basilio, I'm not interested in talking cuisine."

"Bear with me, please. I am more than a restaurant owner. There is a reason my places serve the finest Cuban food in the world. It is because I go to great lengths to make sure I have the finest chefs and staff. I help coordinate, sponsor, and extract the best people out of Cuba."

"What do you mean?"

"Besides being a restaurant owner, I'm also in the immigration business. To be blunt, I export/import Cuban chefs that have a desire to leave their repressive homeland and cook in the greatest country in the world. America."

Nigel had to stop and process what he just heard. He took a long drink of rum and said, "Smuggle. You smuggle chefs out of Cuba?"

With a smug smile, Basilio said, "I prefer the word export." Then he laughed and continued, "Can you think of a better, more excellent import for our country?"

Nigel said nothing.

THE CUBAN

"While many are destroying this country by importing massive loads of shit from China, I import only the best Cuba offers. It is a win-win for everybody, and I quickly learned it is impossible to teach a Bob or Joe the proper ways of a Cuban kitchen."

"How do they get here?"

"By boat. Are you aware of the wet foot, dry foot policy?"

"I've heard of it, but never had reason to study details."

"Long story short. If a Cuban migrates to America and can place their foot on U.S. soil, they can stay and apply for legal residency after a year. While at sea, they consider them a wet foot. If intercepted by the authorities on the open seas, our government will return them to Cuba, where certain harsh punishment awaits them."

"Thanks for the little policy brief, but let get to the bomb, please."

"Patience, my friend." He took a long pull on his drink before continuing with his story. "Our worthless president, with his hand-holding compassion for the Castro regime, is planning to end the wet foot, dry foot policy. That would make any Cuban that enters the U.S. illegally subject to deportation."

"Well, let's just be honest, my friend. Doesn't that make sense?"

"Nigel. It was the U.S. government that created the Cuban Adjustment Act in 1966 to give the oppressed people of my country an opportunity to escape their land and start a new life in this wonderful world. It has been a U.S. policy that has given my people hope for a better and free life. Now the president wants to kiss up to Castro and take it all away. Why would that be fair?"

"Okay," Nigel said. "We have set a long-standing precedent. I get it. What the hell does that have to do with a damn bomb on your boat? I'm still waiting for that part."

"My contacts in Cuba help me identify the right candidates that want to leave. Not every chef qualifies. They must be exceptional. I have my standards, you know. When I got word that Alvaro and Isabell wanted to leave Cuba, I had to work fast. I wanted them to have a dry foot status before a policy change. My prior exports were not so difficult. When you know all the right people, things get done. This one was tricky because of the security."

"Why would that be?"

"Because Alvaro isn't just an exceptional chef. He *was* the personal chef to Raul. Not anymore," he said with a grin.

"Raul... as in Raul Castro?"

He said nothing, but lifted his eyebrows.

"You're shitting me, right?"

"The Cuban government has known about me and my operations for years. They have their spies in our country. Don't think they don't." He knocked back the rest of his rum and reached for the bottle. As he poured a fresh glass, he said, "This time... things have gotten personal."

"So, the guys I saw on your boat were Cuban operatives."

"That is why I took Alvaro and Isabel to New York. They will be safe there. The Cuban community will see to it, and my friend in New York has already started the proceedings with U.S. immigration. After their year is up, they will come to Miami and work for me."

"That is an amazing story, but if those guys want you dead, I can't see them stopping in their efforts."

"You are right, my friend. That is why we must find them first."

"Are you saying you know who it was that came for you?"

"Not exactly, but we have ideas. We have our spies too."

"What are you going to do?"

"Say goodbye, my friend." He laughed and said, "For real, this time. No kidding around. I can't stay here and put the rest of you in jeopardy. I must go into hiding for a while."

"When are you leaving?"

"Immediately and don't ask where."

"Will you be back?"

He stood, escorted Nigel to the door, and looked around the marina. "You'll know soon enough."

What the hell was that supposed to mean?

Basilio turned and gave him an enormous hug that almost squeezed all the air from his lungs. He let go. As Nigel coughed to catch his breath, Basilio said, "Help me cast off."

"You're leaving now?"

"The sooner the better, my friend."

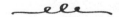

Nigel stood on the dock and watched as *Cubano Freedom* made its way toward the channel. Basilio gave his air horn three long blasts and waved from the flying bridge. Just like that, after such a long time of threatening to leave and never doing so, he left. An emptiness filled Nigel's soul, and sadness rushed in. It was all so sudden and crazy. All he could do was think of what he had once said. *We do whatever needs to be done.* Then he turned to head toward *MisChief*.

After a few steps down the dock, his phone rang. It was a wet-netter colleague, letting him know the mullet were running thick at Jetty Park. Out of instinct, he turned his head to look toward the bay. Jetty Park is the spit of peninsula that separates the marina basin from St. Joe Bay and creates the channel. One way in. One way out. He was only a few short minutes away.

"Really?" he said, welcoming the convenient distraction. "Save me a spot on the wall."

"Wishful thinking," said his friend. "Word is spreading fast. You better move your ass."

He ended the call and increased his pace. If he didn't hurry, he'd be competing with every wet-netter in Gulf County. Fried and smoked mullet is a local favorite, but fishing for mullet isn't done with a rod and reel. It takes the skill of throwing a cast net to haul in your bounty. His cast net is always in the back of his truck, waiting and at the ready for such short notice. Now he was running.

THE CUBAN

Back in Virginia, they only use mullet as cut bait, not as main fare for consumption. They consider people to be mighty desperate to catch them to eat. So... you can imagine his surprise when he discovered so many affluent people on the Forgotten Coast were so damn desperate. Turns out, here, the desire to catch and eat mullet spreads across all social classes, for good reason too. Because they are so freak'n tasty! Folks back on the east coast don't know what they are missing.

When his truck skidded to a stop, he was lucky. He had gotten there in time. Plenty of guys stood along the seawall, nets made up, eyes all focused in one direction, but there was room for more. As he grabbed his five-gallon bucket that contained his net, he heard someone yell, "Stand by, boys. Here they come. They're all balled up this time."

Nigel turned and watched the progression of throws as the nets took to the air. There is something special about watching all those nets get tossed and open wide like pancakes over the water. *Splash! Splash! Splash! Splash!*

"Save a few for me, bitches."

They ignored him.

He took his place on the wall down the line from everyone else, being the last one to have a chance of filling his net, but he wasn't really interested in catching over five or six. He planned to fry up a couple and smoke the rest at the house. "How often are they making a pass?" he asked the guy ahead of him.

"About every three to five minutes. They are all over the place. One school might be six, the next sixteen, and the next sixty."

"Sweet."

He stood with his net, made up and ready to go. There was no great need to focus on the water ahead of him. He would get plenty of warning as soon as the nets before him hit the water, so he let his eyes wander over the bay. He smiled as he caught the distant stern of *Cubano Freedom* steaming out of the bay. *Fairwinds, my friend.*

From down the line, he heard, "Pay attention! Here we go."

The throws and splashes began. Nigel waited. He didn't see any at first, but kept his eyes peeled. Then a small school of stragglers came into view. He let them pass and launched to catch them from behind. As he pulled in his net, he felt the tugging struggle of the captured. When the net emerged, he had two nice ones. *Perfect. A couple more like that and I'll be set.*

He cleared his net and dropped the fish in his bucket. They flopped around, drumming the beat of panic until he reached in and broke their necks, to put them out of their misery and bleed out. After rinsing his hands in the bay water, he went back to the methodical procedures of getting the net ready for another throw. Looking around, he noticed someone standing up by the road and looking out over the bay. He grinned. It was Desi, Basilio's friend. He was on the phone talking to someone.

"Hey, Desi!"

Nigel wasn't sure if Desi recognized him, but it was obvious he didn't like being identified like that. He looked Nigel's way, then turned to walk in the other direction. Desi ended the call. After he put the phone in one pocket, Nigel watched as he pulled something from another pocket and stretched an antenna out to full length. *What the hell?*

What happened next surprised everyone. The explosion was massive. A black mushroom of smoke followed the fireball that reached for the sky. Seconds later, Nigel felt the energy from the explosion bounce off his chest. It totally engulfed *Cubano Freedom* in flames. Nigel looked up and found Desi to be gone. Dropping his net, he scurried up the rocks and yelled, "You son of a bitch!"

As Nigel emerged up on the road, all he could see was a black SUV speeding away. He dashed to his truck to make chase. He jumped behind the wheel only to remember his keys were with his net and phone down at the wall. He turned to look for the SUV. It was gone, and he slammed the wheel with his palm.

He got out of the truck and watched the boat, burning out of control in the bay. There was nothing he could do and had never felt more helpless. Collapsed beside his truck, he sat with his back against the front left tire and pounded his fist into the pavement.

After a while, he wondered what he should do. How much should he share with the authorities? He decided he would tell them everything, which wasn't much. But... with Basilio gone, perhaps he had some information that might help bring some justice for his Cuban friend.

His appetite for mullet no longer existed, so it didn't upset him to discover a Great Blue Heron had poached his catch from the unattended bucket. After collecting all his gear, he made his way back to the marina. The walk to *MisChief* seemed long. His legs felt tired and heavy. When he got to his best girl, he slid open the hatch. Something below caught his eye, which then brought a smile and a tear. It was two cases of Havana Club rum, with a brief note attached.

If you can help yourself, my friend, save at least one bottle for us to share when I get back. It may be a long while before we see each other again, so please... exercise some restraint!
Best,
B.V.

Pulling out a bottle and speaking to the note, he said, "I'm so sorry, my friend. Dammit!"

Thirty minutes later, Nigel walked into the Port St Joe P.D. building.

"Can I help you?" asked the receptionist through the front window.

"I hope so. I need to talk to someone about what happened today. The boat explosion."

"Oh... pertaining to what?"

About that time, two officers came in. One was Sleepy, the officer that was on the scene as they took Nigel from *Cubano Freedom*. Nigel looked carefully at the name tag. *Smith.*

"Officer Smith. Nice to see you again. I need to speak with someone about what happened on Basilio's boat. The one that is still burning out of control out in the bay."

"Oh... we just came from Jetty Park. What a mess out there, but we won't be involved. The Florida Wildlife Commission will have the lead on investigating the cause."

"The FWC? What if I say it was intentional?"

"Arson?"

THE CUBAN   65

"No. Murder."

The two officers looked at each other with scrunched brows. Then Smith said, "What are you talking about?"

"Okay," he said, "listen. The guys I saw on Basilio's boat. They planted a bomb on board."

"How do you know this?"

"Because Basilio brought this guy in from somewhere to inspect the boat. A demolition explosive expert. He called him Desi."

Nigel described this Desi guy and explained how he supposedly found a bomb aboard. And later, how he saw Desi at Jetty Park, focusing on *Cubano Freedom* with a device in his hand immediately before the explosion. He did not, however, mention any of Basilio's questionable immigration operations.

"So, you think this fella named Desi blew up the boat and Basilio?"

"Yea! Basilio was double-crossed. Best I can figure, it was probably this Desi guy that whacked me over the head the other night. You need to find that SUV."

The other officer looked at Smith and said, "I guess we should run this by the chief, but it looks multi-jurisdictional to me. This alleged bomber was in the city during the explosion, the boat was destroyed off the peninsula, so that is going to be the county, and the FWC is still going to have the lead on investigating the explosion. If there is anything to this, it will end up with FDLE."

It made sense to Nigel that the Florida Department of Law Enforcement would ultimately get involved, but he was more concerned with the *now*, not *later*. "Guys, we still need to find that SUV."

"Mr. Logan," said Smith, "you haven't exactly given us much to go on here. Just your suspicions and a black SUV? Do you know how many of those are around?"

"It was a General Motors model. Probably a Chevy Suburban. Maybe a Cadillac Escalade."

"That doesn't help much, and you have no tag number."

"No," said Nigel. "I don't."

"Okay," said Smith. "We'll talk to the chief and see how he wants to handle it. We'll be in touch if we need an official statement."

"That's it. That's all you are going to do?"

"Like I said," said Smith, "we'll speak with the chief, and we'll be in touch."

The two officers disappeared behind a door and left Nigel frustrated. He drove the few short blocks to the city boat ramp and several FWC trucks were pulling patrol boats out of the water. One officer was sitting in his truck talking on a phone. He ended the call and rolled down the windows when he saw Nigel approaching.

"Is there something I can help you with?" the officer asked.

"Were you able to get the fire out?"

The officer shook his head. "No, afraid not. There was too much damage, and she was taking on water. She sank as the fireboats were trying to extinguish the flames. Did you see it happen?"

"It was a bomb," said Nigel.

The FWC officer didn't even look up, but he said, "That is how other eyewitnesses are describing it."

THE CUBAN

Nigel wanted to explain that he was more than *just* an eyewitness, but he didn't. He didn't want to retell the story. He already reported what he knew to the police, so it was in their hands now. He thanked the officer and, with a nasty taste in his mouth, headed back toward his truck. Once inside, he opened his console and retrieved his bottle of Jim Beam. After washing out his mouth with a plentiful pull on the bottle, he put the bottle back and stared ahead through the windshield.

CHAPTER ELEVEN

Nigel warmed his stool at the end of the bar to close out the longest day he could remember. He had been there since mid-afternoon, and from the time he sat down, Candice made sure his mug remained charged with beer. Once the clock struck 1800, two things happened. Sailors at sea heard four bells: two quick raps, a brief pause, then two more. It was also Nigel's signal to shift to bourbon.

A couple of hours before closing, a man took up the stool next to Nigel. Nigel turned his head and squinted through his foggy vision to look at the man. The man looked familiar, but he couldn't be sure. Nigel said nothing.

"The folks at the marina said I could probably find you here."

"Those bastards," slurred Nigel, "are always throwing me under the bus." Squinting even harder, he looked at the fella. Then it hit him. He attempted to snap his fin-

THE CUBAN 69

gers, pointed at the guy, and said, "Smith! Officer, Smith!" Then he whispered into his glass of bourbon, as he prepared to finish what remained. "I thought I recognized you."

Shortly after that, Candice brought over the bottle and was about to pour, but Smith put his hand over the glass, and asked, "Do you really think he needs any more of that?"

"It isn't about how much he needs," replied Candice. "It's about what he wants. Now please, move your hand."

He did, and she poured a finger's worth into the glass. She looked at Nigel and waited for him to look up. He finally did and gave her a wink. She looked at the officer and said, "He's fine. Can I get you anything?"

He was off duty and in civilian clothes, so he said, "A pint of Oyster City Blond Ale would be nice."

"Put it... on my tab," blurted Nigel.

"I can't let you do that," said Smith.

Sounding a little belligerent, Nigel said, "Don't tell me what I can and can't do."

Right before leaving to get Smith his beer, Candice said, "See? He's fine."

Nigel didn't pick up the glass. He sat there resting with his eyes closed, trying to pull it together. After a while, he said, "So, did you go looking for that SUV?"

"We did."

Candice brought Smith his beer. After she left, he continued, "And we found it."

Nigel's eyes sprang wide open, and he turned his head and waited to hear more.

"And it seems," said Smith, "that maybe your story isn't so farfetched."

Nigel picked up his glass. He brought the rim to his lips but set it down without drinking. A surge of sobriety flooded his head, and he called out. "Candice! Water and coffee, please. When you get the time."

Smith started by saying, "I probably shouldn't be telling you this, but..." He explained how both the city and the county had stopped several SUVs with no results. Then later, a deputy in a county squad car, sitting at the Raw Bar at Indian Pass, noticed a black Escalade with blacked-out windows roll past, heading toward Franklin County. The deputy fell in behind and followed for a while before pulling the vehicle over.

Smith got quiet for a spell.

Nigel killed the first tall glass of ice water, then said, "And? Go on. What?"

"Well, if it is the same guy, and we have no reason to think it isn't, the person you referred to as Desi is Desiderio Machado. He was driving the SUV."

"And?" Nigel pulled hard on the bitter, old coffee that Candice poured from a pot made earlier that afternoon.

"The driver was very cooperative, and the deputy kept them for a long time while he called in the driver's license and registration."

"Desi, that son of a bitch," scowled Nigel. "Where is he now?"

"That's just it. It took a long while to verify everything with the State Department..."

"The State Department?"

THE CUBAN   71

"Yeah. When the word came back, they instructed the deputy to apologize and let him proceed."

"Wait... Proceed! You fucking let him go?"

"Nigel, both the vehicle and the driver's license are registered to the Cuban Embassy in Washington, D.C. There was nothing we could do. Mr. Machado and the vehicle enjoy the privilege of diplomatic immunity."

"Diplomatic what?"

"Immunity. It means..."

Nigel lifted a hand. "Stop. Dammit. I'm not stupid. I just wasn't expecting to hear that." He felt more sober than he wanted to be at that moment. "So," he continued, "that Desi has been working with the Cuban Government all along."

"That would seem to be the case," said Smith. As he stood to leave, he gave Nigel a pat on the back. "Remember, like I said, 'I probably shouldn't be telling you this...' but given the circumstances, I thought you had the right to know."

Nigel slumped back on his stool and pushed away the refilled glass of water and empty coffee cup. He turned to watch Smith leave, and Candice came to check on Nigel. When their eyes met, she saw his filled with despair. "Everything alright, baby?"

"No... nothing is right. Everything is wrong, and I want rum."

She turned to look at the shelves of bottles and said, "Well, if you feel you must, I have..."

He interrupted her. "No. You don't have what I need. I have plenty on the boat. I need to settle up and go."

"Please, tell me you're not driving. Let me take you."

He shook his head as he staggered off his stool, and on unsteady feet said, "No... my truck will be..." He waited for the room to stop spinning. "... fine parked out front. The walk will do me good."

CHAPTERT TWELVE

At 0400, Nigel's eyes popped open. He was in the cockpit. A half-empty bottle of Havana Club rested on his chest, cradled by his arms. His mind and head felt thick. The result of a full dose of day and night drinking. For a moment, he thought yesterday had been nothing but an awful dream, but he looked across the water to where *Cubano Freedom* berthed. It was gone. He looked below in his cabin and saw the cases of rum. No. It had all been real.

Down below, he loaded his percolator for coffee and put it on the stove. As he waited for that first pot, he sat at the salon table and grabbed a pen and a piece of paper. He scribbled down the name Smith had mentioned, *Desiderio Machado*, and stared at it. He drew a near-perfect circle around the name. The pen kept following the circle around, making it thicker and thicker, until it made a border. Then he did the same, making a smaller circle inside the bigger one. As the kettle of boiling water whistled, he dissected both circles up and down and across with a fine line. Nigel looked at the name as it rested in the hand-drawn crosshairs, and despite his aching head and sorrow, managed a smile.

After the coffee, he pounded down water and Gatorade all morning long. He was badly dehydrated from his drinking shenanigans, and he knew it. He needed a clear head, and pushing fluids into his bloodstream is the best way to cleanse his gray matter and other organs. Fresh air is an excellent remedy too. The flags were flying at the marina. A nice sea breeze was filling in from the southwest and expected to build as the land continued to warm up from the rising sun. It was time to kick *MisChief* away from the dock and go for a sail. For Nigel, there is no better way to rest his brain and recharge his spirit than to let his boat take him away.

The wind direction put *MisChief* on a nice and easy reach, a fast point on sail that kept the boat moving well. She put her starboard shoulder down and tracked well out of the channel toward the tip of the Cape San Blas peninsula. Once clear of the bay, she would have quartering swells to play in to add to the fun, fast sail down the coast. The plan was *no plan at all*. Just coastal sailing, eye candy for beachgoers that had already staked claim to their sandy vacation retreat.

Standing forward at the stem, he used one hand to hold the forestay, while the other steadied his binoculars for a glance at the beach and at what lay ahead. He was sailing on a lee shore, which meant if something were to happen to the boat, the wind and surf could drive the boat ashore. Never good. But he was about a mile out, and that gave him plenty of space to avoid disaster. Besides, he knows

MisChief and *MisChief* knows him, so they both have a vested interest in taking care of each other.

While he was eyeing the shore of St. Joe Beach, a puffing noise and spray of seawater hit his leg and got his attention. The blowhole of a surfacing dolphin sent seawater high in the air, only to land on Nigel. He looked down around the bow of the boat. They were everywhere, playing in the bow wave as *MisChief* surged on. Nigel went aft to go below and retrieve his Nikon, but by the time he got back on deck, they had gone.

He went back to the binoculars and looked down the beach toward Mexico Beach. A steady stream of fishing boats was exiting the channel and heading offshore, hoping to land *the big one*. Whatever that might be. Further west, beyond Mexico Beach, were the pristine, protected waters of Crooked Island and St. Andrew Sound. They were too far away to get a good peep through the glasses, but it didn't matter. Nigel loves that little secluded piece of coastal heaven. As the crow flies, the cut that leads into the sound is about seventeen nautical miles from the marina in St. Joe. They already had a good start, so he lowered the binoculars and reported. "*MisChief*... we have a destination. Make way for Crooked Island. Hold your course, but expect to come up on the wind in twenty minutes."

The approach to St. Andrew Sound was easy. Once inside the protected anchorage, the swells and waves of the Gulf of Mexico ceased to exist. *MisChief* traveled further west into the sound. Two other cruising sailboats had the same idea and were already resting at anchor. Nigel found a nice spot between them. There was plenty of water on each side and a good holding for the anchor.

After stowing the headsail and putting the cover on the main, he squared away the deck and lines. *MisChief* doesn't have a Bimini Top for shade, but she has a rectangular awning that Nigel put up to help protect the cockpit and him from too much sun. Then he went below to open all the hatches so the boat could breathe. After double-checking everything, he thought, *Now I can relax.* The thought made him laugh because, truth be told, he was already more relaxed than he had been in weeks. The short cruise was just what he needed, and he settled in the cockpit to kick up his feet and look out over the water. He felt much better and realized a couple of things as he sat there. First and most important, he hadn't thought about Basilio and his fate since the night before. That was good; those thoughts only hindered his decompression. The other thing, which was basic but fairly important, was the fact he couldn't remember the last time he had a bath. He grabbed his t-shirt and pulled an underarm to his nose. "Ahh, shit. I smell like... crap."

*Fi*ve minutes later, he tossed a bar of Ivory soap in the water and jumped his naked ass in.

He got whistles and catcalls from one sailboat as he crawled up the ladder. He didn't care, even gave his head and backside a little extra shake to shed some water. That brought additional whistles that made him laugh. He grabbed a towel for some cover, gave a wave, and took a seat in the cockpit to dry off. The towel removed most of the wetness, but the rest of him would have to air dry. He was salty, but he was clean and refreshed.

After his sailor's bath and drinking a lot more water, he felt refreshed. Even fantastic. His head was clear. Mission

THE CUBAN   77

accomplished. He got up and went below to put on fresh clothes. Seeing the rum made his brain tighten and eyes twitch. He laughed, then spoke to the cases. "I'm ignoring you, but don't take it personally."

With clean cargo shorts on, he sat at the salon table and pulled close the piece of paper with the written name and drawn bullseye. He studied it and thought of the things he learned from Officer Smith: the U.S. State Department, the embassy SUV, the diplomatic immunity stuff, Desi's ultimate release; the whole thing made him sick. He crumpled up the paper in his fist and threw the wad and watched it bounce around the cabin before coming to rest next to the half-consumed bottle of rum. He grabbed the bottle, ready for a pull, but put it back and picked up the wad of paper. He opened it back up and spread it flat on the table. After looking at it for a couple of minutes, he did a quick Google search on his phone and wrote the phone number for the Cuban Consulate under Desi's name.

"There is no way he has made it back by now," he said aloud, thinking of Desi's trip. St. Joe to Washington D.C. was one hell of a haul. That didn't matter. He was making this up as he went along, so he dialed the number, anyway. The automatic answering system was in Spanish, and he listened intently until he heard, *For English, press one*. He let the Spanish version continue, as it gave him a little extra time to think about his approach. It helped little. When the Spanish chatter stopped at the end of the message, he pressed one on his phone and listened. *For directions to the embassy, press one. If you know the extension of the party... press two. To speak to the operator, press three.* Nigel hit the keypad.

It rang for a long time before someone answered. The voice was in Spanish, but Nigel started straight away with English right after the greeting. "Hello. I need to speak with Desi Machado, please."

The receptionist was quiet for a while, then in her good English, said, "I am sorry, but there is nobody here by that name."

"Yes," said Nigel. "Desi... Desiderio Machado. You must be the new girl, or perhaps you're just not familiar with him."

"I'm sorry. I've worked here for ten years, and I know all the staff. This Desi you speak of..."

Nigel interrupted her lie. "I'm so sorry. This whole thing is so embarrassing. Mr. Machado was in Port St. Joe, Florida yesterday. County deputies stopped him and... this so humiliating... the officer that pulled him over failed to return his embassy driver's license. What a blundering idiot. You can bet your sweet ass we will discipline him. Oh, I'm sorry about the language..."

Now it was her turn to interrupt. "Sir. What did you say your name was again?"

He was quite certain they had a Caller ID system that revealed his name, so he just confirmed what she already knew. "I didn't. Sorry for being rude. My name is Nigel Logan. I was just..."

She interrupted again. "Please stay on the line while I connect you with someone."

Nigel smiled as his awkward conversation with the receptionist was replaced with Cuban music. Again, the wait was long. Nigel imagined the discussions going on as they figured out who was going to talk to this lunatic on the

THE CUBAN

phone. Finally, the music stopped, and someone asked, "How can I help you, sir?"

Nigel grabbed a pen. "Who am I speaking with?"

The guy didn't answer the question. "What is your business with the Cuban Embassy, sir?"

"I'm not sure I have business with the embassy," said Nigel, "but I do with Mr. Machado."

"Mr. Logan, you have already been told. There is no Desiderio Machado here at the embassy."

"And that would make you a fucking liar. How do you feel about that?"

There was more silence on the other end. Then the embassy staffer said, "Well, *if* there *was* such a person here, what would your business be with Mr. Machado?"

"If... If!" Nigel pretended to lose his temper. "Why don't you stop playing games? I hate games. So, after I hang up with your worthless lying ass, call Desi and let him know I have a message from Basilio Valdez."

The Cuban staffer said nothing.

"What's wrong? Cat got your tongue?" said Nigel.

"Well, perhaps this Mr. Valdez should try to contact this Mr. Machado himself."

"That would be impossible now, wouldn't it? Just deliver the message, asshole."

Nigel ended the call, sat back, and wondered what he had accomplished. He reached for the bottle of Havana Club and got a glass out of a cabinet. As he poured a couple of fingers, he said, "At least I got their damn attention."

CHAPTER THIRTEEN

He enjoyed his day of swinging on the hook so much he stayed the night. While he was sure the other two boats were running generators and air conditioners, the sea breeze and awning kept the heat of the day tolerable. He used to think installing an AC unit would be smart, but not anymore. A unit would require valuable space. Space not readily available on an old classic sailing yacht such as *MisChief*. Plus, he has seen the result of such creature comforts on other boats. They hold owners and crew hostage below when it gets a little hot. The two boats around him were proof positive. The dinghies of both boats were back from the beach and not a soul was visible on deck.

It was late afternoon, and his diet had been Gatorade, water, and rum. He was getting hangry, a combination of hungry and angry. He checked his stores and found plenty of canned beans. There was quite a variety: navy, black, baked, and butter. He grabbed a can of black beans. It would not be a very glamorous meal, but that was sort of his style. Keep it simple. It is only fuel. He checked the refrigerated icebox and found four bottles of Coors Light in the corner and plenty of water. The Gatorade was long gone.

He went back on deck to get in the shade. *It would be a perfect meal*, he thought. *What more could I ask for?*

About that time, he noticed a gorgeous, tall bathing beauty emerge from down below on the boat anchored closest to him. She walked along the side-deck amidships and noticed Nigel watching. In her tight little bikini, she threw up a friendly wave and dove off the side. As Nigel waved back, he said aloud, "Well... there is that."

He felt quite refreshed the next morning, having kept the previous night's private party modest. There were only two empties of beer in the trash, and he put a responsible dent in the bottle of rum. What started as half-full, he reduced to about a third. He was on his second pot of coffee and used it to wash down his breakfast of leftover black beans. He soaked up the quiet, sitting in his cockpit, waiting for the sun to make its appearance. One of his favorite times when on the water. He was in no hurry and had no agenda. Not until later, anyway.

Nigel took his time and tinkered around the boat. The cooler temps of the morning gave him an opportunity to rub in a coating of linseed oil to his teak handrails and cockpit coming. While most sailors avoid brightwork at all costs, what they end up with is crappy-looking trim that soils and promotes growth of unwanted mold and other organisms. All it takes is a little time and diligent effort to maintain the woodwork on a boat. Nigel takes great pride in the way *MisChief* presents herself, and her brightwork is one of her best visual qualities. A classic sailboat, properly maintained, will always stand head and shoulders above the plethora of plastic and stainless-steel productions being produced today.

Once he finished his morning chores, he had worked up quite a sweat and a cool swim was in order. The shallow, sandy, clear-water shoals of Crooked Island were only about twenty-five yards away. The deepwater rises quickly to make a large shoal, often populated by scores of powerboats that anchor there on day trips. None had arrived that morning, but it wouldn't be too long before the watercraft started showing up.

Diving in, he surfaced and rotated to start a backstroke toward the beach. Nigel made effortless strokes and powered his six-foot-three-inch, two-hundred-thirty-pound frame across the top of the water. When he noted the change in the water's color, he knew the shallows were beneath him. He kept stroking, but he stopped when he heard a boat motor come to life. Nigel gently put a toe in the sand, hoping not to find a stingray, before standing. It was one of his neighbor's dinghies. A guy was piloting the inflatable easily toward Nigel. Nigel threw up a wave, just to make sure the guy saw him. The guy waved back. Communication made.

As the guy got closer in his approach, he killed the motor and coasted. "Morning," said the guy with a smile.

THE CUBAN

"Morning back at cha," said Nigel as he noted about six mullet that schooled along the bottom.

"It's beautiful," said the guy.

Nigel spread his arms and waved them around. "It doesn't get much better than this."

"You are right, but I was speaking of your boat."

Nigel turned to look at and admire *MisChief*. She rode handsomely at anchor. A breeze held her, so they could have a broadside view of her starboard topsides. The morning sunshine cast a favorable light on her hull and rigging. "Thank you. But don't say that too loud. She already feels mighty full of herself as it is."

The guy laughed. "Pearson Vanguard, yes?"

"That's right. She's a sixty-six."

"I grew up sailing on one. My father had a sixty-three. Seeing yours brings back some splendid memories. He died when I was eleven, and my mom sold it after about a year. I wish she would have held onto her, but mom was never crazy about sailing, anyway." He stopped to gaze at *MisChief* for a while and continued. "She doesn't look a day past one."

Now it was Nigel's turn to laugh. "Well, I don't know about that, but the years have been pretty good to her."

"Hey, you don't mind if I go putting around her so I can get a better look, do you?"

"Have at it. Go aboard and peek below if you like. Just be mindful of the brightwork. I just finished oiling the teak."

"Thanks, and I know. I saw you working her. I appreciate it."

The guy pulled on his little outboard and eased away. They never introduced themselves to each other, which is a simple thing to forget when talking about boats. Nigel smiled and returned to his swim.

He stayed at it for about an hour, only stopping for short rests and to stretch his shoulders that were tightening. It had been a long time since he used swimming as an exercise, and he had forgotten about all the other muscles that seem to get omitted when working out in the gym. Swimming will make you remember them.

His watch read 1038. It was time to go back to work, so he made his swim back to the boat a fast one. After toweling off and plopping down in the cockpit, he grabbed his phone and hit re-dial. He listened and worked his way through the automated system until the receptionist answered with a live voice. He was sure it was the same gal. "Hey, morning. Me, again. Has Desi Machado gotten back yet? I sure would like to get this license back to him. He must have had a fit wondering where it is?"

She wanted to call him out on his bullshit, but couldn't. She knew the license angle was an act. The embassy had spoken with Desiderio the day before and knew his license was in his possession, but... they maintained that Mr. Machado was not part of the staff. She bit at her bottom lip. Then said, "I'm sorry. No such person works here."

"That's okay, sweetheart. As usual, you have been a superb help. When you see him, let him know I'll buzz back later."

"That, sir, won't be..."

She slammed down her phone.

He had already ended the call and gotten up to grab one of the two remaining beers. The last one he would

THE CUBAN   85

save for when he got back to St. Joe. It was time to make
preparations for getting underway.

CHAPTER FOURTEEN

The sail back to the marina was easy and uneventful. The winds were more westerly, and once far enough offshore, he could crack off his heading and reach all the way back to St. Joe. *MisChief* did it all on one tack with just a few sail trim adjustments and course changes. Easy shmeezy.

He walked into the City Bar late that afternoon to find his buddy Red and his wife, Trixie, in a mild confrontation. They were at the bar, so Nigel joined them. Red was looking through a catalog, studying images. Candice brought Nigel a Coors Light with Lime, and said, "Here ya go, baby. One Coorsona."

He ignored the *baby* reference and looked at Trixie. "What's going on, Trix?"

"Nigel, I'm glad you are here. I think Red has completely lost his marbles."

THE CUBAN

Nigel laughed. "You're just now figuring that out." He looked past Trixie to get a better look at what had Red's undivided attention. "Whatcha got there, buddy?"

Trixie answered for him. "He thinks he wants a tattoo."

"A tattoo? Red, what the hell are you thinking?"

"That's the million-dollar question," replied Trixie.

Without taking his eyes off the pages of potential designs, Red said, "Don't give me any shit. I've always wanted one."

Trixie looked at Nigel. "He's never mentioned it. Not once."

"Red," said Nigel, "what's brought on this recent infatuation with ink?"

"All the cool kids are doing it," said Red. He stopped and slid the book of artwork their way so they could see. "What do you think about this one?"

It was an image of Jesus hanging ten off a surfboard with a large, curling wave breaking.

"Red. You're sixty-one years old," Nigel reminded him.

He snatched the book back and kept looking. "What the hell does that have to do with it. I'm still hip."

Trixie rolled her eyes.

"Look at this one." And he slid the book over. It was of a tramp-stamp that said, *Take me to the party,* with little bottles used as quotation marks.

"No, Red," said Trixie.

Red frowned, then turned the book to a page he already had dog-eared. "I really like this one."

The image was an actual picture of a tattoo. They inked and labeled a propeller on each cheek of some dude's ass. The left cheek said, *Port.* The right cheek said, *Starboard.*

Nigel laughed and said, "Hell, I'll pay for that one, if you promise to keep your pants up."

Trixie slapped Nigel on the arm. "Dammit! Don't encourage him!"

Nigel winced with a smile and said, "Okay. Okay. Just trying to help."

"Hey," said Red, "that's an idea. One cheek could say *Help* and the other *Yourself*."

Trixie's eyes were burning into Nigel's. "You're not helping, so get up and leave."

Nigel slid off the stool, laughing. "Okay. Have it your way. I have a phone call to make, anyway. I'll be at the end of the bar if you need me."

"Not likely," she scowled.

Like before, Nigel hit redial. After hitting the key for the receptionist, the phone seemed to ring longer than before. He was sure they were studying the Caller ID, wondering how to handle him. Candice brought him a fresh beer, and he had all the time in the world, so he waited. Several minutes later he heard the call get answered, followed by the familiar sound of a call getting routed elsewhere. Nigel smiled. After another couple minutes, a familiar voice answered the call without a welcoming, *Hello*. "Mr. Logan, I don't know how many times you have to be told, but no Desiderio Machado works here."

"Ahhh, it's you again," said Nigel. "So good not to have to explain myself repeatedly with someone new."

"Mr. Logan, we don't have time for your games. We are busy, and..."

THE CUBAN

Nigel interrupted in a sharp and serious tone. "Fuck you. I'm the one that doesn't play games, but when forced into them, I usually win."

"You are harassing us, and it will stop."

"Listen up, scumbag. I know who Desi is and what he has done. I'm guessing you know, too. Otherwise, you wouldn't be covering for him. So, here is the deal. You need to let that shithead know..."

The call ended. Nigel smiled, took a sip of his beer, and under his breath said, "It will take more than that to get me to go away."

A little over an hour later, Nigel was getting ready to leave. He settled his tab with Candice and was collecting his truck keys off the bar when his phone rang. It was from a 404 area code number and not in this contact list, so he dismissed the call and let it go to voicemail. Didn't give it another thought.

It is a short drive back to the marina, which is why he usually walks into town. He was listening to his, and everyone else's, favorite radio station, Oyster Radio out of Apalach. He put the truck in park and listened as the sole owner and disc jockey, Michael Allen, was giving the weather forecast, which was called for heavy thunderstorms into the evening and continuing through the late morning hours. "Probably a good night to stay at the cottage," he said, looking at the radio dial.

After buttoning up the boat, Nigel walked back to the truck with his partial bottle of rum. He heard thunder in the distance. Michael was right. Weather was coming, and as Nigel pulled into his gravel drive, the first splattering of rain danced on his windshield.

He looked for something to eat and decided on soup and crackers. Thinking of Candice, he laughed, because he didn't have any other choice. But it would be fine. While heating the soup, he noticed the notification light blinking on his phone. It was a voicemail from the earlier call. He tossed the phone down and said, "Later."

The cottage has a great little screened-in porch out front. With the soup bowl empty and pushed to the side, he sat back and relaxed as the light rain developed into a steady downpour. The distant thunder was closing in, as was the wind, which caused the rain to blow in through the screen and dampen Nigel. He collected his rum and phone and moved to the dry side of the porch. He loved to porch sit in the rain. Setting his gear down, he saw the notification light still blinking. He grabbed the phone. It was a voicemail. *Crap.* He recharging his glass with more rum before listening to the message.

Mr. Logan, my name is Stewart Kohl. I am with the U.S. State Department out of the Atlanta office. I'm calling about recent calls being made to the Cuban Embassy. They, the embassy staff, feel you have been harassing them, and I wish to discuss the matter with you. Please return my call at...

Nigel ended the recording and deleted the voicemail before saying, "Screw you, Stew."

The next two days went about the same. He called the embassy on a schedule, once at 1000 and after lunch around 1300. Each time, the phone rang without the receptionist answering. Well, she did, but she ended the calls

THE CUBAN   91

as fast as she answered them. There was no more direct routing to some angry staffer that he could poke at. It was frustrating, but probably more for them than Nigel. He kept up with the calls, if for no other reason than to drive them crazy. He had also deleted, without listening to, the additional voicemails left by Mr. Kohl from the day before.

The next morning, the winds were perfect. Nigel went for a short sail in the gulf. He came back in mid-afternoon, and, on his approach to the slip, noticed a man standing on the dock. He stuck out like a sore thumb, wearing a dark suit and wingtips. He had removed his coat, and it hung over his arm. *Hmmm. Interesting. A suit in Florida.* As Nigel got closer, he could see the guy's white shirt drenched in sweat and stuck to his skin like glue. The guy never waved. He just waited and watched as Nigel tied up the boat. When finished securing *MisChief*, Nigel said, "You're a little over-dressed, don't cha think?"

"Mr. Logan," the guy said unamused, "I am Mr. Kohl with the state department. I need a word."

Nigel thought, *You got to be kidding me*, but said, "Looks like you need a beer. Come aboard. I'll get you one."

"No thank you, Mr. Logan. Could we go up to the café so we can speak?"

Nigel almost declined just to keep the suit in the sun, but thought better of it. "Sure. Hold on while I get myself a beer. Sure you don't want one?"

"No, thank you. I'm on duty."

"Stew, you're not in Kansas anymore. We don't play by those rules down here. When in Rome..."

"No... please come along."

As they walked into the air-conditioned space, Nigel killed off the rest of his beer and tossed the empty in the trash. Walking to an open booth, he spoke to the bartender, "Hey Tee! Please bring me the usual and a large glass of cold water for my friend."

Mr. Kohl fell into his side of the booth and said, "We are not friends."

"That might be the case, Stew, but down here, we have a reputation of being friendly. You might try it. It will get you a lot further than you can imagine." Nigel paused for a beat or two and continued, "So, tell me. Why is it a hot-shot G-Man from Atlanta travels to Port St. Joe to speak with me?"

"I think you know why I'm here."

They both got quiet as Tee approached with the drinks. After setting them down, she said, "Sorry, Nigel. We're out of limes. But I'll give you this instead." She reached down and kissed him on the cheek, then flashed a wink at the stranger.

When she was out of hearing distance, Mr. Kohl said, "You have to stop harassing the staff at the Cuban Embassy."

"I don't have to do any such thing. You... you can't bother the Cubans. You're the gubment. I am just a simple citizen with no ties to law enforcement. They list the number on their website, so I call."

Kohl said nothing, but frustration was written all over his face like a billboard.

Nigel jumped in with both feet. "They have a guy. His name is Desiderio Machado. He's an agent, a staffer. I'm

THE CUBAN   93

not sure what the hell he is, but they deny he works there. You and I both know that is a lie."

"You have to stop."

"He killed a man. A friend of mine."

Kohl looked the other way to regain some composure, then looked at Nigel and said, "You're speaking of Mr. Valdez."

"Yes, so you're famil..."

"You have no proof, Mr. Logan."

"Screw you. I saw the whole thing. Machado was on Basilio's boat. He's some demolition expert or something. Minutes later, I saw Machado with a device in his hand. He detonated the bomb he put on the boat."

"I'm sorry," said Kohl. "Sorry for your friend, but that isn't enough. Plus... they enjoy diploma..."

"Just shut up. Don't say it like that. Like it's a privilege they get to... enjoy!"

"Like it or not, it is the truth. They are not willing to cooperate and there isn't much that can be done."

"Don't give me that bullshit." Nigel stopped and looked into Kohl's eyes. He saw nothing. There wasn't any compassion to be found. "Wait," said Nigel, "you guys don't want to do anything about this. You guys don't give a fuck."

"We care, Mr. Logan, but about different things. Mr. Valdez isn't who you think he is."

"Was, asshole. Was!"

"Your friend has created an enormous strain on our relations with Cuba."

"Relations? What relations? Oh... that's right. We are all touchy-feely with Raul these days. I almost forgot."

"It is more complicated than you can imagine."

Nigel wanted to tell Kohl that he knew everything. That he knew far more about Basilio and his operation than Kohl could ever imagine, but he didn't. He remained angry and steadfast in his convictions. "I think we are done, Stew. You've given your little speech. Now beat it and enjoy your drive back to Atlanta. Don't gas up here in town. You'll pay tourist prices. That's just a little friendly advice."

Kohl stood and took one last drink of water, then said, "Let me give *you* a bit of friendly advice."

Nigel said nothing.

"We know who you are, Mr. Logan. We know why you are here in this sleepy little coastal town. You are still under investigation in Virginia." Kohl now had Nigel's full attention. "Yes. We know everything. If you don't stop with your calls. I am quite certain we can convince the FBI to cooperate and intervene with the Virginia authorities to help bring that case to a close."

Nigel said nothing.

"I take from your silence that we have an agreement."

"I did nothing wrong."

"Well," said Kohl, "I guess that *could* be something for a jury to decide. Have a nice day."

Nigel sat, looking forward. Anger brewed deep within. After finishing his beer, he slammed his fist onto the table. "Son of a bitch!"

CHAPTER FIFTEEN

Nigel drove his truck through town. His phone alarm went off, and he grabbed the unit and quieted the chime. Then he scrolled through his recent calls, found what he was looking for, and hit re-dial. With the speakerphone on, he pressed all the prompted keys, which at this point had become automatic, and tossed the phone on the passenger seat. There was no reason to wait for someone to answer. Once the ringing stopped, he glanced at the phone and thought, *Assholes*. Not really paying much attention to the road, Nigel nailed a pothole. Through his rear windshield, sliding glass window, he heard a groan and some selective cuss words. Nigel turned his head toward the rear window while keeping one eye on the road and said, "Sorry, 'bout that."

"The hell you are," came the reply.

"You know, Red, this is going to put me on the Trixie shit-list. You know that, right?"

"She doesn't have to know immediately."

"I hate to be the one to tell you, but she already knows. In case I haven't told you lately, you're an idiot."

"How the hell did she find out?"

Nigel said nothing.

"Anyway, you're the one who paid for it, so who's the idiot now?"

After a few days of considering his options, Red decided on the butt-cheek propellers and spent almost five agonizing hours on the tattoo artist's table. Nigel didn't stay there the entire time, but he stuck around long enough to enjoy the sneering and growling as the artist's needle worked over Red's derriere. Nigel asked the tattoo guy, "Are all your subjects this much of a puss?"

The tattooist grinned without answering, and Red howled from the table, "Go tooooo hell."

Nigel walked around so he could look his friend in the face.

Red said, "No pain. No gain."

Nigel chuckled and said, "I understand the pain part. The gain part... not so much." Nigel looked up at the tattooist and said, "I'll be back in a while. Remember, the word *port* should be colored red, *starboard* needs to be green."

"Got it."

As Nigel left, he noticed Red's stuff sat on a table. It gave him an idea. He walked over, picked up Red's phone, and took a picture of him on the table. Then he texted it to Trixie. Feeling quite pleased with himself, Red's phone gave him another idea, so he slipped it into his pocket.

In the truck, he had both phones in his hands. One he read from; he used the other for the call. When that familiar voice of the receptionist answered, Nigel said, "Good to hear your voice again."

"Excuse me?"

"Have you forgotten about me already? I thought we had some good chemistry working. Anyway, hey…"

"Mr. Logan?"

"Yes. The other day I got this interesting visit from the U.S. State Department…"

Click. The call ended.

Nigel put the phone down saying, "Y'all are no fun."

When Nigel returned to collect Red, he was still laying on the table. "Is he all done?"

"Yup. He is going to need to keep it well hydrated. I recommend Palmers Cocoa Butter Formula with Vitamin E. It…"

Nigel held up a hand to stop the speech, then used his thumb to point toward Red. "Dude, I am not the guy you need to be telling this to. I'm not sure who is going to spread cream or butter on his ass, but it ain't me."

Nigel tilted his rearview mirror so he could better see the truck bed. Red looked like a beached walrus back there on his belly. "It's gonna be a while before you can sit. Are you sure you don't want me to take you home so you can lie down?"

"No, dammit! I want a drink. City bar. Pronto."

Nigel couldn't help but laugh as he watched his friend scooch his way out of the truck. He stood with an awkward stance. He tucked his butt cheeks in and poked his hips forward. Anything to help keep his baggy shorts from rubbing up against his new art. Watching him walk was even funnier. As they approached the front door of the City Bar, Trixie came out to meet them with a not-so-friendly welcome. She pointed at Nigel and said, "You, sir, are on my shit-list."

Nigel turned to look at Red and said, "See? I told you."

"You," Trixie said, a rigid finger pointed at Red's nose, "have a lot of explaining to do. Now get your ass inside."

Red winked at Nigel as he eased his way forward. "She's just crazy about me."

"Yeah... I can tell."

Nigel pretended like he was going to slap him on the ass, which caused Red to panic and bellow out from the expected pain and poke his waist out even further.

"Damn you, Nigel."

"What are friends for?" Nigel looked at Trixie and said, "I'll leave him in your good care. I'm going after some oysters."

After a couple beers and a dozen raw at the Seaside Cafe, Nigel felt like a nap and strolled down the dock to *Mis-*

Chief. He poured what remained of the bottle of rum into a glass and sipped it in the cockpit before laying down in his v-berth. It was Florida hot, but his Windscoop was deployed above the forward hatch, which really helped funnel fresh air down into the boat. Five minutes after shedding his clothes, he was sound asleep.

When the boat moved, he didn't give it much thought. But when the salsa music filled the cabin, his eyes opened. He lay there listening when he heard a distant booming voice chatting away in frolic banter. Nigel sat up. He twisted his body to get out of the v-berth and came face to face with the barrel of a gun. That and one of the mystery men from the dinghy that night astern of *Cubano Freedom*. It was the face he vowed to never forget, and he kept his word. "What are you doing here?"

The man said nothing.

The music continued as they stared at each other for what seemed an eternity. "Y'all killed him. My friend is dead."

Still, nothing came from the man holding the gun.

"For what? Why?"

Nigel stared into the stoic expression on the man's face. There was nothing more from the Cuban.

"You son of a bitch. Talk to me!"

When the man failed to utter a word, Nigel lunged forward and was met with gunfire and bullets.

As Nigel clutched at his chest, he sat up quickly and slammed his face into the boat's overhead. He fell back, holding his nose. He was drenched in sweat and panting. He tilted his head up to peek into the salon. It was empty. There was no guy. There was no gun. There was no salsa music, only the memory of a vivid dream. He fell back and rubbed his head.

The dream bothered him throughout the rest of the afternoon. He did inane chores about the boat to help occupy his mind. Once finished with the second freshwater wash-down, he sat on the dock to drink beer and watch the boat dry. He was hot and sweaty, but a nice breeze puffed across his face and cooled his skin. He closed his eyes to enjoy the moment and wait for the next little gust. It came and with it a hunger pang. He looked at his watch. It read 1723. "Damn," he said aloud. "Those oysters didn't last long."

The City Bar is on speed dial. When Candice answered the phone, Nigel asked, "I gather it is safe for me to come over?"

She laughed, "Yeah. All clear. Trixie took Red home a couple of hours ago. It's funny. She made him drive, so he'd have to sit on his ass."

"Hey," said Nigel, "I'm hungry. What about you? I know you haven't left the bar all day."

"Oh, Mr. Logan, I am. Are you asking me out on a date?"

"I'm asking if you are hungry. Thinking about picking up some fried chicken or catfish from the Pig. Would you like me to pick something up for you? Or, if you prefer, I can always heat something from my fine selection of soup."

THE CUBAN

"Nope. Piggly Wiggly catfish with mac and cheese sounds great."

"Hushpuppies?"

"Of course, stupid, that is a given."

Nigel showed up with dinner, and they ate at the end of the bar. She had to take quick bites and nibbles between taking care of patrons. The fried catfish from the Pig is always superb.

From Nigel's stool, his perspective and view of what was happening behind the bar were unobstructed. Kenny Chesney's song *Save It for a Rainy Day* was pumping out of the sound system, and Candice swung her hips and danced as she pulled beers and poured drinks. Her tan legs and body were showcased by tight-fitting, cutoff blue jeans and a sleeveless t-shirt that had the bottom scissored away to show just enough of midriff.

He didn't realize she caught him staring until it was too late. She started a sexy saunter his way. He couldn't take his eyes off her hips and the hypnotic way they moved from side to side. It wasn't until she stopped and leaned forward so their eyes could meet that he realized he had been busted. He jumped back with embarrassment. His beer mug went flying off the bar and his tray of catfish overturned. After a few moments, he looked up. She was right in front of him. "I'm sorry," he said. "It's just that..."

"You find me irresistible?"

He said nothing as his face filled with blood and color.

"That's what I thought."

She turned and walked away with the same sexy strut. He said, "Stop that, dammit..." after a pause he added, "later."

She turned and winked.

When the place filled up with locals, the fun and games were over. Candice was too busy for her normal shenanigans with Nigel, but still used her sex appeal with the other male patrons. She pulled Nigel a fresh, cold beer and brought it to him. "It's crazy tonight," she said before turning, pointing at a guy, and saying, "Whatcha having, sweetheart?"

After several hours of hustle and bustle, things were settling down. Nigel looked at the clock on the wall. It was 2150, approaching 10:00 pm. Candice made her way over to Nigel and put her head on the bar.

"I'm exhausted," she said.

"Hell... I got tired just watching you. You never stopped, like the Energizer Bunny."

She lifted her head to look at him and offered a smile as she bit on her lower lip.

"Well, I better get going. It's been a crazy day for me too. I need some rest. Let me settle up."

"Nothing to settle up, hon. Beers on me. You brought dinner."

Nigel looked at her Styrofoam container of cold fish. "You've hardly eaten a thing."

"It will heat up fine in the micro." She leaned in and snuck a quick kiss to his lips. She wasn't fully confident, but she was sure he put a little effort into kissing her back. "Thanks. Be safe walking back to the boat."

As Nigel stepped off the stool, he quickly realized just how much he had consumed throughout the evening. A little stumble to the right was offset by a wide stance to

THE CUBAN   103

catch himself and stay vertical. His forward progress required a bit more concentration to maintain a straight line.

Once outside, the fresh night air hit his lungs, and he instantly felt better. He started his stroll toward the marina then something made him in his stop in his tracks. The brake lights of a black SUV flashed down the street before making a right on First Street. He shook his head. *Black SUVs are like damn squirrels*, he thought and continued. As he was crossing Second Street, he stopped again in the middle of the road, eyes forward. Then he looked to the right. There it was again, stopped in the middle of the intersection on Williams Avenue. Nigel started walking toward the SUV, but as he did, the driver stomped on the accelerator and sped away, squealing tires. Nigel kicked off his flip-flops and picked up his pace to a full run down the street. He ran as fast as he could and almost fell as he made the right turn on Williams. He got there just in time to see the SUV had made a left on Third and was speeding away. He kept running in pursuit. Not because he thought he could catch the car, but because he had picked up the sound of running feet behind him. They had lured him down Second Street into a trap.

Nigel was fast, but being barefoot brought the chase to an end. After crossing Long Avenue, Nigel stepped on a rock and twisted his ankle, falling and rolling on the pavement. When Nigel stopped, he was face down. The guy chasing stood straddled over Nigel and leaned down and grabbed him by the back of the shirt. Nigel rolled to his right and delivered a fist straight to the guy's groin. The guy gave out a dry moan and released Nigel to cover and protect his jewels. Nigel struck again, and the guy's hands did little to protect him as the sound of cracks and snaps indicted newly broken fingers. The guy stepped away, folding over at the waist. Nigel jumped to his feet and balanced himself the best he could with the bad ankle, then went into attack mode. The guy saw Nigel coming, and he stood straighter to charge at Nigel. When the guy was close enough, Nigel delivered an open palm strike just below the guy's nose and followed through with a reach for the heavens. Nigel felt the guy's facial skin rip away from the skull, and his septum cartilage tear away just before the nose broke. The guy dropped to his knees. Nigel stepped in and grabbed a hand full of hair to help keep him upright. He was just about to hit the guy again when the black SUV came screeching around the corner. Nigel tilted the guy's head back and came down with another punishing blow. As the guy fell face down, Nigel turned to wait for the SUV.

Nigel was in the middle of the street. They could have run him over, but the driver slammed on the brakes and stopped right in front of him. The driver's side door opened and out came Desiderio Machado. He had a gun pulled, but Nigel didn't care. "You son of a bitch! There you are!"

Nigel charged and landed a solid right hook to Desi's cheek. The Cuban stumbled a bit, but kept coming, yelling, "Stop! Stop!"

But Nigel didn't. Like a bulldog, he rushed in with a left, but it was blocked, and Desi answered with a right of his own. Nigel and his bad ankle went to the ground. As he scrambled to get to his feet, Desi pointed the gun and said, "Would you just stop! He's alive, dammit."

"No!" yelled Nigel. He wasn't willing to listen to anything this guy had to say. Now on his feet, Nigel did his best to limp toward Desi. That's when the passenger-side window rolled down and a familiar voice said, "Are you taking good care of our rum?"

CHAPTER SIXTEEN

Nigel stood with his mouth open, disbelieving what his eyes were telling him. It was impossible. He looked at Desi and said, "Shoot me now, so I can wake up from this dream."

"It isn't a dream, Nigel. It really is me, Basilio."

Nigel's head snapped over to look at the guy in the passenger seat.

"Yes," said Basilio with a smile. "It really is me."

Nigel looked over at the guy that had been chasing him, now punished. Desi was helping him to his feet.

"Nigel. My friend. Look at me."

He did.

"We can't stay here. Please get in before the cops show up. I can't be seen. To those that have an interest, I am dead. I must stay that way. Please get in."

Nigel ran around to the other side and opened the door so Desi could help the poor fella get in. Then he ran back around to jump in on the other side. When he opened the

THE CUBAN   107

door, he saw something in the third-row seating that made him pause. Then he jumped in. As soon as he shut the door, Desi hit the gas, and they sped away.

Everyone was quiet for a spell. The Escalade had worked its way around town, and they were heading west on Highway 98. As they were crossing the canal bridge, Nigel asked, "Who are the guys in the back seat?"

Two figures sat upright and quiet in the back. Their hands were zip-tied behind their backs, as were their feet. Black hoods covered their heads, drawstrings tied snugly around their necks.

"Ahh," said Basilio, "Those are two of our friends that you chased off *Cubano Freedom*."

Nigel reached over and pulled on one end of a drawstring to untie and loosen the hood. He grabbed the top of the hood and jerked it off. It was the guy from the dinghy and his earlier dream. Duct tape was stretched across his mouth. Nigel looked at the guy and they exchanged glares. Then Nigel took the hood off the other guy. Nigel didn't recognize this one. He certainly wasn't the second guy in the dinghy that night. Nigel gazed into the guy's eyes and said, "Basilio, you say these are the guys from the boat that night?"

"That would be correct."

Nigel reached back to feel the back of his head where a huge knot once took residence. Then he balled up a fist and... *Whack! Whack! Whack!* "Nice to meet you, asshole!"

By the time Nigel hit the guy a second time, Basilio turned to see Nigel holding the guy by the shirt and pounding his face. Desi grinned as he watched through the rearview mirror. Blood poured from the guy's nose, and he was out cold.

"Don't kill him, son," said Basilio. "He has vital information we need."

"Where is the third one?"

"That is part of the info we need to get from him. That and other details."

Nigel sat back in his seat. He looked over at the guy he beat up. "Dude, I'm sorry. Really."

The guy said nothing and nodded his head.

Turning his attention back to Basilio, Nigel said, "Do you mind telling me... what the hell is going on? I saw Desi detonate your boat."

"Yes, you did," said Basilio. He turned to look at his friend. "We weren't expecting you to be there to see that. Oh... and please put the hoods back on our guests. They should stay in the dark for now."

Nigel did as he was asked, and Basilio continued, "Raul wanted me dead. So, while we avoided my ultimate demise, we thought it best to make Castro think he had been successful. Desi rigged the boat himself. Once I got close enough to the end of the peninsula, I put the boat on autopilot, collected a few personal items in a plastic bag, and slipped off the stern. Once I got to the beach, I called Desi to let him know it was okay to proceed."

"But you blew up your boat. Your beautiful *Cubano Freedom*. That had to be tough."

"Ah yes. That was tragic for sure, but she was only a boat. There will be another *Cubano Freedom*. Mark my words. What would have been truly tragic is if those cases of fifteen-year Havana Club had been left aboard."

THE CUBAN   109

"That's why you put them on my boat."

"Of course. There was no way I could swim them to the shore. Plus, I need to travel light."

"I finished my first bottle earlier today," Nigel confessed.

"Then you started with your calls to the embassy. That was another wrinkle in our plan. Nigel, you placed way too much emphasis on Desi."

"So, Desi. You do work for the embassy?" asked Nigel.

Desi nodded his head as he drove.

"Yes," said Basilio. "He works for the embassy, but his true allegiance is with the real Cuban people, not the government. I told you, we have our spies too."

Nigel said nothing and listened.

"The embassy believes our friends in the back handled the explosion. Your calls to the embassy created confusing suspicions about Desi. We hoped you would just stop, but you didn't. That is the reason we came back for you, to get you to stop."

"I'm sorry. I just..."

Basilio raised his hand to get Nigel to stop. "It's okay, my friend. You felt you were doing what needed to be done." He shifted his focus to Desi and said, "Anywhere around here should be fine."

Desi slowed, and Nigel looked around. They were in Mexico Beach. Desi turned down a road and found a vacation rental that wasn't occupied. He pulled into the drive, parked, and turned off the lights. Basilio turned sideways in his seat and looked at Nigel. "I hope you don't mind, but this is where we say our goodbyes, again. I know you are a resourceful person and can make your way back to St. Joe."

"Of course," said Nigel.

"We have to get a move on. We have a lead on the third guy. He is in Destin, and Knuckles and Chuckles back there are going to take us to him." There was silence before he continued, "So, let's get out of the car so we can say a proper goodbye."

They met at the front of the vehicle. Basilio pulled Nigel into a massive embrace, once again squeezing the air out of him, and said, "Thank you, my friend. Thank you for caring and for trying to help. The best thing you can do now is nothing. We have it from here."

Basilio released Nigel, and he coughed to regain his breath. "There is no reason to ask when you will be back, is there?"

"No, but I will. After all, you have my rum."

"Ahhh, my rum, bitch. Possession is 99% of the law."

Basilio laughed and said, "Yes. I guess it is."

"What about the guys in the back?"

"There are hungry sharks where they will be going."

"Won't it cause more suspicion if they go missing?"

"It won't be the first time Cuban operatives come to America and decide to disappear into the fabric of this great country."

Desi rolled down his window and called out, "Basilio. We need to go."

"Enough said," said Nigel. "Come here and give me one more hug."

He did, but this time it was Nigel that got the first big squeeze in. Basilio followed suit, and it became a competition of who could squeeze the hardest. After a long while, they both gave up and laughed. Nigel watched his friend

THE CUBAN

get into the car. Desi didn't hesitate with the departure, and just like that, Basilio Valdez disappeared for a second time.

Nigel stood there and looked around before walking back toward the highway. He pulled out his cell phone and dialed a number. When the party on the other end answered, Nigel said, "Wake up, Red. Get out of bed. I need a lift."

Nigel listened to his friend bitch.

"I don't give a shit about your ass. I'm in Mexico Beach. Put your new props in gear and come get me. I need to get home."

All Nigel heard was *blah, blah, blah, blah.*

"You can sit on two pillows for all I care." Then he realized his approach with Red was all wrong. After two seconds of thought, he shifted his tactics to exploit Red's one true vulnerable weakness. "Red, if you can be at Mango Marley's in less than an hour, there is a bottle of fifteen-year-old Havana Club rum in it for you. The real shit."

Through the phone, Nigel heard his buddy bellow in agony as he scrambled to his feet before ending the call. He looked at his watch, marked the time, and thought, *Forty, forty-five minutes... tops.*

The End

THANK YOU!

If you enjoyed *The Cuban*, there are a few things you could do to make this author incredibly happy.

First, provide a short, honest review at Amazon. Those reviews mean so much more than you could imagine. It doesn't have to be long. We appreciate *star only* reviews too.

Second, if you like Nigel Logan and the gang, please consider signing up for my monthly newsletter. There, you will gain some insight into Nigel Logan and the knucklehead that created him. Oh... That would be me. PLUS! You can grab a **FREE** copy of *The Cuban*, a Nigel Logan novella I wrote just for you. And... If you join us, I will make you this one promise: *I will not fill your inbox with junk and SPAM*. Sign up at www.KirkJockell.com

THE CUBAN

And the third thing is, contact me. I love to hear from readers. Let me know what you thought of the book. It would make my day more than you can imagine.

Email: Kirk@KirkJockell.com
Facebook: www.facebook.com/KirkJockellAuthor
Website: www.KirkJockell.com
Instagram: www.Instagram.com/kirkjockell
Book Bub: www.BookBub.com/Kirk S Jockell

ACKNOWLEDGMENTS

My most sincere appreciation goes out to so many people. None more so than my wonderful wife, Joy. She is my bride, my partner, my rock, and number one supporter. To do things without her would be impossible. Her love and encouragement are nothing short of amazing.

During my journey as a writer, my friends (old and new) mean so much to me. They provide the greatest support imaginable. There are too many to mention, but you know who you are. Thanks so much! You help to keep the engine running.

And I would be remiss if I didn't mention my special writing partner, sniffer of butts, and canine shenanigans: Nate. He always seems to know the perfect time (by his clock) for a break, a walk around the hood, and a belly rub (his not mine). Thanks, buddy, for keeping it real.

Then, there are the folks that keep me from looking *too* stupid, which isn't easy. That I can promise. The editing

THE CUBAN   115

and proofing team: Jan Lee, Tim "Coach" Slauter, and
Gretchen Douglas. Thanks, guys. We did it again.

Getting emails from readers is one of the best parts of
this job. Thanks to all of you that have done so. They
are more valuable than the royalties. *And hey, I like the
royalties... a lot!* Words cannot express the appreciation I
have for each of you. Thanks to you all!

About the Author

Kirk Jockell is an American writer and the creator of The Nigel Logan Action Series. Port St. Joe, Florida is home, but he sleeps most nights in Flowery Branch, Georgia, where his wife continues to work one of those regular day jobs she loves (Yuck). He patiently awaits the day she can join him in retirement and trade it all in for a simpler life back down on The Forgotten Coast. Kirk is a sailor and an avid photographer of sailboats. He loves to fish, throw his cast net for mullet, listen to music (Pop Country doesn't count), play his guitar, and drive his Bronco on the beach. Kirk lives with his lovely wife Joy, a rescued bluetick coonhound named Nate (#98Nate), and a tuxedo cat named Mr. Hemingway.

OTHER WORKS BY KIRK S. JOCKELL

The Nigel Logan Action Series

The Tales from Stool 17 Series
Finding Port St. Joe (Book 1)
Trouble in Tate's Hell (Book 2)
Dark Days of Judgment (Book 3)

More Nigel Logan Books
Tough Enough (Prequel)
Tupelo Honey (Book 4)
Traffic (Book 5)
Tidewater Moon (Book 6)
Tormented (Book 7)
Trapped (Book 8)
The Cuban (Novella)

Made in United States
North Haven, CT
06 May 2024

52143467R00075